No More Water

No More Water

Hugh Arthur

Hexford House

Published by Hexford House

www.hexfordhouse.co.uk

Publisher's Note: This is a work of fiction.
Names and characters are the product of the author's
imagination and any resemblance to actual persons,
living or dead, is entirely coincidental.

ISBN: 978-1-9164173-0-4

1

R A I D

There is a reason that the drug squad turns up at the dealer's house at 6am and knocks the door in. If it sent a letter one month in advance to announce that it was coming, when the day arrived there would be no drugs to be found. Similarly, on a late summer day in Üsküsdar, three representatives of the Turkish Business Commission Special Investigation Unit arrived early at Jeder's office before Hakan, Hakan's assistant or Jeder. There was no overnight security guard on duty. Mehmet had dismissed him the previous week for taking stationery out of the office supplies cupboard without permission and allowing his dog to roam unleashed around the kitchen. Interviews had been conducted to recruit a replacement but Mehmet had found fault with some aspect of each of the three applicants' character and he had decided to take the risk over the first weekend to leave the building unguarded. Mehmet's Friday had been consumed by his preparations for the Monday meeting with the olive oil producers and he did not want to be flustered into rushing or staying late before the weekend to interview three more prospective candidates.

So the Special Investigation Unit waited patiently until the first employee arrived. Other than with their bare fists, the Unit did not have the means to knock down the front door, its representatives just wanted to be directed to the Chief Executive's office where they would wait until he arrived. Mehmet, Jeder's boss, would normally be in before him but today had left for the Aegean coast for that meeting with the olive oil producers.

It was eight o clock on a Monday morning. Jeder had arrived half an hour earlier than usual to research and prepare olive oil price estimates for the coming year, a task he had casually deferred from the previous week. He would need to talk to people in the Ayvalık office, but with Mehmet about to dominate proceedings there all day, that was going to be impossible. Jeder's earlier departure from his house that morning had reduced his travel time by ten minutes. He really did have the best commute in the world. A twenty-five minute drive from Europe to Asia, against the traffic. He surveyed the Bosphorous from the considerable height of the second bridge, viewing Ottoman houses that were finally beginning to be restored after years of neglect; and, more imposingly, massive oil tankers

2

chugging back and forth along the great waterway connecting Russia to the rest of the world.

Already seated in Jeder's cramped office were the three SIU representatives, smartly attired in business suits, white shirts and sober ties. All three men sprang to attention on his entrance. The spokesman was a tall man in his early forties who stooped apologetically when gesturing his colleagues to exchange handshakes with the Mancunian. The younger of the other two men, who observed but initially said nothing, was quite handsome with a dark complexion and an immaculately groomed moustache. They tried to remain anonymous for as long as possible. The tall man carried a briefcase while the other two each carried an attaché-case; Jeder wondered how many relevant papers to his case each bag contained. Or perhaps they were all empty in the hope of taking away documents from his office. Jeder felt sure he would not release anything without Mehmet's prior permission even if the representatives provided a search warrant. The bags all looked light, like in films when actors pretend to hold full tumblers of coffee or laden suitcases but you can see quite clearly from the way they are being carried that they are all empty.

Jeder rehearsed the business continuity plan clauses for kidnapping, extortion and general business disruption. These instructions were provided for employees' safety in the event of an emergency. They had been prepared by an American consulting firm before translation into Turkish and they were safety-first measures, meaning employee security first, company security second. This wasn't a kidnapping but it could be an extortion. Mehmet would be sure to view it as an irritating diversion caused unnecessarily by Jeder. Jeder studied the features of the front man and decided that he at least would not be asking for money. If he didn't possess the authority then that decision would pass to his superiors. The front man was here at the prescribed time at the appointed place, confident in his right to be there, well within the law. Exactly as his boss had ordered. It would be straightforward.

Jeder wondered why they were sitting in his narrow shared office full of Hakan's paraphernalia and Hakan's assistant's files. They could all have been assembled in Mehmet's offices, around the meeting table with the bolt upright dining room chairs. Better still, they could have all convened in Hussein Yıldırım's building across the Bosphorous in Levent. Hussein Yıldırım had the whole of the 12th floor given over to a meeting room; even lunch arrived from another floor. Hussein Yıldırım was so important that the partly constructed Istanbul underground railway was going to have one of its first station stops in Levent, although Jeder doubted

4

that Hussein Yıldırım would ever travel by the tube except on the inaugural trip with the Prime Minister and other important dignitaries. Perhaps there had already been a meeting in Hussein Yıldırım's suite on the 12th floor or maybe already one with Mehmet in the Üsküsdar office and this was why it had been convenient for them to arrive on a day when they knew the senior manager was working away from his office; this was all to test Jeder, how he would react, what he would say, he thought.

The phone rang; it was unusual unless one of his staff had arrived early and wanted to come and see him. It couldn't be Gail – she only rang him at home and she rarely wanted anything or needed to speak to him. The same with Mehmet, he would always ask someone else, considering them to be more reliable. The boys never called him – what an ineffective parent he had been. He picked up the receiver, there was a delay and an echo of background noise before the confident and familiar broad baritone of Nurettin, calling from abroad, announced:

'I have some good news from Spain, I have found our engineer.......a water engineer. Exactly the person we have been looking for.' How Jeder hated it when Nurettin used the collective, as if he had any influence in the design or execution of the grand plan, but for sure he knew he would be implicated at the time of its downfall. Jeder delayed his reaction....he was expected to be as impressed as if Fatih Terim had just signed the top-rated Italian international goalkeeper for Galatasaray.

The three men from the SIU who had previously sat motionless suddenly took more interest when Jeder relaxed into his phone conversation in an upbeat mood. 'That's good, well done, we needed him'. They concentrated on parts of Jeder's face, avoiding staring as that would be considered effrontery.

'He has great expertise in management of reservoirs', Nurettin's voice was very clear, although the surrounding fax connection-like electronic sounds gave the impression he was calling from a satellite in space.

'Good'. Jeder knew Nurettin would be affronted by such a curt response. Jeder was so enthusiastic about this project.

'He has 'history'', Nurettin wanted to settle in to a long conversation now the line atmospherics had become less obtrusive. He always made an optimistic comment about his project so Jeder couldn't possibly have thought that Javier had spent time in jail.

'What sort of history?' Jeder freed the tangled phone cord from under his desk and turned away from facing the SIU staff to look out the window, hoping that the investigators would afford him some privacy. There was a high concrete perimeter wall only a couple of metres away outside - its monotony broken only by ivy tendrils and other small weeds.

The front man began to shift awkwardly in his chair as if he had encountered a stray tack protruding through the mesh in a dangerous area. Jeder felt embarrassed that he couldn't have found three good seats in his room for visitors. They could have gone to Mehmet's office but whoever accompanied them into the building and up the stairs had decided that they should wait for Jeder.

'Let's call it 'tarnished''. Nurettin relished the adjective as if it was some form of elaborate embroidery and proud that it was an impressive word from his English vocabulary.

'This new recruit is a real capture'. Jeder joked as he turned away from the window and cast his eye around the room, wishing he had tidied it before he had left on Friday. There were piles of soft folders, individual letters, contracts, all supported by thick computer print outs – Emin would for sure be calling for those that morning, expecting them to have been reviewed and signed off.

'I can't wait to meet him, when are you back?' Jeder hoped he sounded distracted.

'*Don't* sound so excited. What you say....when a horse falls from heaven you don't inspect its teeth, no! He has family history in engineering, his father was well known in Valencia. We need his strong credentials.'

Almost on cue Emin, armed with two more large printout files, suddenly appeared in the doorway to the office, no doubt encouraged by the commotion he could hear from down the hall. The three men who were facing Jeder craned their necks to see who had attracted his attention but they did not rise. Likewise, Emin fixed his stare on Jeder and didn't acknowledge the visitors.

'He's *not* his father', Jeder suddenly felt the urge to douse the conversation; he couldn't ask how this water engineer was going to contribute to the project from Spain, whether Nurettin was going to pay for him to move, or if all his costs would be funded by 'Jeder's money', or indeed if there *was* any other money as Nurettin had continually reassured him.

'You'll see', Nurettin volunteered optimistically. At this point the tall man stood up and gestured loudly at the phone with a perfect English accent 'Please!' Jeder didn't realise that he was in a mosque and needed to respect silence.

'Who is telling you *please*?', Nurettin growled from Madrid. All his enthusiasm had evaporated as the last word of the sentence was spoken in a deep bass, about an octave lower than the first, the electric plug to the turntable fusing. Jeder could envisage Nurettin in his hotel room with his right hand already rummaging deep into his black curls finding the right spot to massage his cranium, something he always did at the first hint of exasperation when events weren't going entirely his way.

'It's Emin', for the first time Jeder engaged Emin with eye contact.

'Just tell him to go away'.

Emin couldn't have heard Nurettin but probably imagined what he'd said and, speaking across the telephone conversation, excused himself, 'Shall I come back later?' and left, not waiting for any reply, undermining Jeder's authority.

'I'm going to have to call you back later', Jeder raised his voice even though the line was by then perfectly clear.

Nurettin could tell Jeder wasn't going to be expansive for whatever reason so he went straight to the point. 'You're late this month with the payment, what happened?'

'Perhaps I can call you back this afternoon', Jeder, for the first time worried that the SIU might be able to hear the loud voice at the end of the phone line, pressed the receiver hard against his ear. He was hopeful that the hesitancy in his voice would satisfy Nurettin. However much Nurettin barked at him Jeder was never physically afraid, such was their perceived disparity in strength; Jeder was slightly taller and in reasonable physical condition for his age. He was self conscious enough to worry that his receding hairline, which he combed back with lotion to keep the dwindling strands in check, made him look older than his 39 years. He needn't have fretted; his pale and still youthful-looking face, with some skin blemishes that betrayed an acne attack in his teens, meant that he nearly always appeared to be the youngest person in the negotiating room since he arrived in Turkey three years previously. Although the onset of a slight paunch warned him he was a once-accomplished athlete starting to go to seed, in his early twenties he had been agile enough and sufficiently proficient to have played outside- half for Waterloo. This accomplishment was lost on Nurettin, who never warmed to Jeder's attempted explanation of the rudiments of rugby union. He related more easily to Jeder's boasting that his game was based on elusiveness, trickery and evasiveness; but the thread was lost again when Jeder tried to explain how somebody aged only twenty-three had to give up because he was already starting to run slower and kept being caught in possession by swift flankers.

For the first time Jeder was glad that the representatives from the SIU were planted in his office; even Nurettin wouldn't want to place part of his funding operation in unnecessary jeopardy.

'I'll call back at 4, make sure you're there and available'. Nurettin's command was repeated in a clear echo and then the phone went dead. Jeder dropped the handset back into its holder. The front man sat down again, gingerly to avoid the tack, but happy that he wasn't required to apply any physical restraint.

It wasn't as if Jeder hadn't thought over the weekend about what he was going to say to Nurettin when he discovered that the payment hadn't reached his account on the previous Thursday or Friday. He was more immediately preoccupied with the fact that the front man was aware of how easily he lied.

Jeder was finding it increasingly difficult to bend to Nurettin's demands, expected to behave like an unquestioning lackey. It wasn't the process of the fraud, which had been simple enough. It wasn't even a huge amount of money involved. Mehmet's company would hardly notice. Jeder's contribution was so minor that Nurettin shouldn't have missed it for a month. Jeder had a tacit understanding that Nurettin was secreting amounts several times higher than that from his French bank employers and, in addition, there were a hundred other people like him feeding the machine; a posse of bookies' runners all obeying their Master's whim. The ultimate objective of damming and diverting the Euphrates for further financial gain didn't sit comfortably with him at all.

As the SIU team continued to silently regard him, looking for signs of weakness, desperation or guilt, Jeder went through the options of why he had been targeted. For a moment he recalled an incident from two weeks earlier. There had been an office dinner in a large house some fifty minutes drive east of Üsküsdar, further into Anatolia. No spouses, partners, boyfriends or girlfriends were invited to such occasions; even the large international hotel restaurants in the Beşiktaş area struggled to accommodate and cater for 100 people, let alone 200. Half the staff lived on the Anatolian side so there was always going to be one half of the office inconvenienced by a long trip home after the office function, whether it was hosted on the west or east side of the city.

It was midweek, Jeder was tired and until he left the party no one else could. So, after saying goodbyes, he prepared to set off at about 11.15pm convinced he could he find his way back to the second Bosphorous bridge. Five minutes into the drive Jeder didn't recognise the road and thought about retracing his steps back to the large house. He turned the car around at the next junction with the intention of returning to the house, but soon came across an exit onto a bigger road which he felt sure would feed trucks from Izmit towards the dual carriageway leading to the bridge. There were no street lights, but from his car's own headlights on the way ahead he could see an obstruction in the road; there was a damaged Toyota Avensis positioned sideways in the middle of the road and several people milling about, but most significantly there were two bodies lying on the ground next to the car.

As he drew nearer he could see that one of the prostrate women was surrounded by a pool of blood and two men, who were wandering around disoriented, on seeing the headlights of Jeder's car, began waving frantically for him to stop. Jeder panicked, aware of his linguistic and cultural shortcomings and the fact that he had been drinking, but at the same time perversely reassured by some casual cocktail chat 3 years previously with an American who had been serving with the US Air Force at Incirlik. At a social gathering in Adana after only a few weeks into his assignment, amid a discussion about newly arrived foreigners immersing themselves into Turkish society, Jeder was provided with advice along the lines of 'don't stop if there is a road traffic accident, you will become embroiled, implicated, even indicted, you'll end up in court...drive on'. He slowed initially to about 30 km/hr, but when he saw that there was a small raised area beyond the roadside, not too steep nor inhospitable, he forced down the accelerator pedal propelling the car forward. One man tried to run into his car's path and then when he saw it was travelling too fast kicked the door and slammed his fist on the roof, shouting '*Mankafa*'. Soon the men's gesticulations in his rear view mirror disappeared into darkness as Jeder made off into the distance. He couldn't return that way and had to keep driving until he reached Sapanca before stopping the car and deciding what to do next. He felt sure that one of the people would have seen and memorised his car's licence plates. They could have been important people with influence; even if not, they could have notified the police. What happened if one of the women had died? Bad advice from the American maybe, but Jeder was the bonehead for following it. This was probably why the Special Investigation Unit was there.

It had seemed like an age but when Jeder gazed down at his watch he saw only a quarter past eight. It wasn't unusual that nobody had rung since Nurettin. He didn't have a lot that other people wanted. Deeply conscious of his own appearance in his Prince of Wales Check double –breasted suit, Jeder was determined to look confident, in control and business-like, even though the very presence of the SIU precluded him from doing any business. He tried to imagine if there were any different actions he could have taken in the previous week to avoid or anticipate this raid. Somehow, even though the front man had said he had asked for Mehmet, he felt that they really did want to see Jeder, and so it was not unnatural that they should be parked in his office. Jeder could hide behind his own lack of authority to not be able to co-operate with them.

He was confined to his office but unable to perform the most rudimentary activity. By rote, each Monday morning the first task he would undertake would be to link up his new laptop to the company's hard drive to capture the work he had performed during the weekend, but this morning he was prevented from so doing. Not that any new information had been added to his computer over the weekend. On Sunday, instead of researching and justifying his olive oil price estimates for the forthcoming year, he had spent the first part of the day on a boat. At dawn he'd driven over the Bosphorous to depart from the Kanlıca ferry station. He'd paid the boatman double the usual rate for an early start to avoid the crowds on a beautiful August day. He asked to be taken down to the Golden Horn and all the way back to the Black Sea and the captain threw in breakfast for a few more million Lira. Bored with his own company before midday he had asked the captain to drop him off at the *iskele* at Sarıyer where he lunched alone at the most packed quay-side fish restaurant and then spent the rest of the afternoon walking back to Emirgan. Another precious Sunday had gone.

'You can talk to your colleagues from the office in this room if you need to. You can invite them here', the handsome man spoke for the first time, trying to make Jeder feel more at ease, talking in English, concerned that Jeder was not being at all industrious. He looked quite pleased with himself as if Jeder might assume that, as he was allowed to speak, he might be on the same level of seniority as the front man. Jeder just thought that the three gentlemen didn't want to be accused of preventing him from doing some work.

'What, can't I leave the room?' Jeder replied in English, giving himself an unfair advantage, and he wasn't particularly concerned that this might appear rude.

'No, you can wait in here, you can talk to people in here, but you can't remove any documents or files or your computer', the front man cut in to assert his position in the group.

'Can I offer you tea, you probably don't want American coffee?

'No, thankyou', the front man declined, on behalf of himself and his colleagues; the government agency he represented must have had a policy that they did not accept any gifts from suspects, lest they be construed as bribes. Jeder began to wish he hadn't arrived at his office so early. He wondered why the person who must have greeted the SIU at 07.30 that morning did not bar them from entering his office. If Mehmet had been in the office that day then he could have dealt with this. It began to dawn on him that it could actually be him that they really wanted to see. As one of the few non-Turks, or at least the only western European, in the company, perhaps it was going to be more revealing to review his activities as there would be more likelihood of extraneous dealings or tainted transactions. Would it be such a surprise if they wanted to determine why he needed to provide Nurettin with US$ 10,000 every month? That was quite an internal affair that he thought he had ring-fenced, unless he had made the mistake of underestimating Mehmet yet again. Mehmet could have devised a system to track exactly what Jeder was doing from the moment he signed his contract, partly out of curiosity but mainly out of distrust.

At twenty past eight Jeder heard people coming into the office, women's voices – two women carrying bags coming up the stairs. He recognised Azize's voice. Azize was Mehmet's assistant. Even though Mehmet was not going to be in the office that day Azize was very elegantly and formally attired for someone Jeder imagined was not yet in her thirties. Her own office adjoining Mehmet's gave her an elevated status, as it was far bigger than most of the managers' offices. She had her own fiefdom, supervising drivers and a whole range of employees and if she summoned anyone to Mehmet's office they had better not loiter.

Seeing Jeder's and Hakan's office door open she came by to deliver a polite morning greeting. When she put her head around the door she could tell from Jeder's expression, the fact that she didn't recognise the three gentlemen and that she couldn't recall that Jeder had scheduled a meeting this early, that this gathering was a surprise. 'Can I provide you with some refreshments?' and then she repeated it for the SIU in Turkish and asked them whether they needed anything else, eager to have some business being transacted rather than have four grown men sit around doing nothing. The fact that Jeder's desktop was bare, apart from a closed laptop, and the three men had no papers nor files in front of them, gave her the impression that all of them had either just arrived or were waiting for someone else to join. The Unit's representatives quickly stood up in unison and politely acknowledged Azize. 'They don't want tea thankyou, Azize'. Then the front man answered her the same way in Turkish, before he switched to English, addressing Azize.

'We are waiting to see Mr. Sunay'.

Azize cast a disdainful look at Jeder before she moved into his office, assumed a position standing next to his desk chair as if in solidarity with him and addressed the front man 'I am sorry, but Mehmet Sunay, the Chief Executive, will not be coming to the office today, he has a meeting with the

Berkem Group in Izmir. He will be returning to Istanbul tonight and will be in the office tomorrow.'

The front man nodded in acknowledgement. He gestured his two colleagues to mobilise themselves, gather their briefcases and attaché-cases, and then made towards to the door. He said a few sentences in Turkish to Azize, reducing Jeder to child status; Jeder thought it was an explanation of the organisation the men were representing, why they were there, why the visit had not been successful and that his superior would be in touch with Mehmet later that day about the next steps. He misguidedly congratulated himself that there was only one sentence that he couldn't catch. Jeder quickly moved to stand between the front man and the exit to the stairs giving him an opportunity to repeat in English what he had said to Azize.

'We will be in touch with Mr. Sunay to provide him with a list of our requirements', the front man summarised, hoping Jeder would understand that there were some sentiments given that didn't require translation and then, gazing down to the level of Jeder's shins, 'Thankyou' as a polite request for Jeder to unblock his path to the stairs. Jeder stood back letting them walk by and he kept a mildly puzzled expression in case any of the three men looked back at him as they left the building, while Azize returned to her office. He heard them leave the building.

Jeder walked over to Azize's office to try to explain what had gone on but found out that she knew as much as he did and she was full of questions about the next steps. 'So they didn't take any papers or files? What about the reputation of the company? Will there be an inquiry? Mehmet *Bey* will not be pleased?' Jeder saw that she had the calling card of the front man on her desk, the same one he had left on Hakan's desk for Jeder as he went out.

'Do you think they wanted to see Mehmet or me?' Jeder replied. Although Azize was younger than him, graded below him in the firm's personnel lists and rewarded less, she assumed a superiority on account of her status as Mehmet's assistant. Although she was seated and Jeder was standing, her self-assurance enabled her to take the higher ground. Azize glared at him expecting a response from him first to at least one of her questions.

'Well I can provide them with the information they requested but I didn't think it was appropriate to do anything until Mehmet was informed. They had quite a lot of information already that they were asking me to verify.'

'I will call Mehmet *Bey* as soon as there is a break in his meeting with Berkem'. Azize wanted to cut their discussion short. 'I can tell him. He should have a break at 10.30,' and anticipating Mehmet's unfavourable reaction she concluded, 'I think it's quite serious'.

Jeder returned to his office with his tail between his legs. As he quickly consulted his diary, to re-confirm the meetings he already knew about that morning, he berated himself for failing to find any elegant answers for Azize.

Even though he knew Azize would be discreet, and not tell anyone, except Mehmet, about the SIU visit, it was possible other people would have seen the men emerge from Jeder's office and would be speculating about the purpose of their visit. Jeder kept a low profile that morning, hardly venturing from behind his desk. He asked the participants of the two meetings he had to come to his office, rather than gather in booked meeting rooms. This meant a suffocating and crowded setting as extra chairs had to be dragged in and awkwardly inserted in the gaps between Hakan's and his assistant's desks. One colleague repeatedly asked why they were not convening in the meeting room and, once no answer was forthcoming, he tried to joke that Jeder liked the colour of his own wallpaper too much. The wallpaper being a series of area maps of different sales regions of Turkey, with red markers signifying the towns in which Mehmet's company was represented, either with its own staff or yellow markers for agents. Jeder was regularly out of the office and used these maps to plan and justify his excursions.

In the afternoon Jeder heard Azize starting a telephone conversation 'Mehmet *Bey*' and he moved over close to the entrance to her office to overhear her briefing Mehmet on the Special Investigation Unit's visit to the office. No doubt Mehmet would be following this up by calling his contact at the Special Investigation Unit to receive his version of events directly. Jeder waited in his office for Mehmet's call. By 3.55pm that hadn't materialised and soon Nurettin would call him.

At that moment Emin stood in the doorway of Jeder's office. 'I had one or two questions to ask you about those payment approvals, is this a good time?' Jeder's heart skipped a beat, as it did every time Azize came to him saying Mehmet would like to see him without saying for what reason. In a sweat he would try to rationalise that by defrauding Mehmet's company but passing all the fruits of the felony directly to Nurettin that his own crime would be mitigated somehow. He wouldn't be able to avoid being cast as the schemer and the accessory to the theft. Neither would Nurettin be exonerated.

Jeder thought if Emin had found the fraudulent instruction he'd better hear about it now then he could tell Nurettin almost immediately that one of his income sources was about to be stopped, 'You'd better come in'.

Somehow in that procedure well over a year before, Jeder had managed to add the name of Içecek Holdings as a commission agent for all Ozel olive oil business. Hakan had completed the paperwork and surprisingly Mehmet had approved it. So when the previous year's annual supplier list came to Mehmet for confirmation he rubber-stamped it, remembering this recent addition. Nevertheless, Jeder felt nervous that this year's list would be reviewed by Mehmet with more scrutiny.

Initially, Jeder had wanted to remove this supplier after the first 0.5% payment had gone successfully through the entire business process, but the explanation and the approvals required to unravel this deceit seemed more problematical than leaving it unchanged. A lot of 0.5% payments to Içecek Holdings had passed through in the meantime. Içecek Holdings was a very similar name to Içecek Oil Holdings which had been a long-standing but now defunct supplier. In fact, 15 months down the line, US$ 180,000 had been paid to Nurettin, masquerading as the long-standing commission agent.

'Jeder, what about the Ozel case?' as if sitting down in the chair opposite Jeder's desk gave Emin carte blanche to talk about anything he wanted.

'Which Ozel case?', Jeder was always amazed that Emin seemed to know almost as much as Mehmet about what was going on.

'You know these Special Investigation people, they are not always the brightest ones'. Emin was always offering a hand of friendship but was continually spurned by Jeder. Here was another chance.

'I don't think you have anything to fear from them', Emin continued, although Jeder had not yet fully engaged, preferring to prepare his first statement once the fictitious supplier was revealed.

'You know how you qualify for the Special Investigation Unit?' There was no answer from Jeder but Emin kept going anyway.

'You must not take alcohol, you must be quite religious and especially, ...you must *fast* properly'. Still no call from Nurettin nor Mehmet.

Emin continued: 'The ones who have English and French languages, they are the ones who stand guard outside until they become bored and leave the service'. It would not require the bright student who had always been top of the class to find the simple deception that Jeder organised each month; the diligent and persistent journeyman would be able to spot it as well.

There was too much risk in having to confide in Emin, if provided with a snippet of information he would quickly work out what was happening and Jeder couldn't palm him off with the ruse about exceptional market price fluctuations. With an Armenian heritage betrayed by his surname, Emin himself was already an office outsider even though he did everything he could to feel integrated. His colleagues represented him as a bigger pariah than even Jeder. As soon as Jeder had arrived three years previously in Turkey Emin identified him as a kindred spirit. He had always stuck out his neck for Jeder right from the first day; going with him evening after evening in his first few weeks to find a suitable property and introducing him to his favourite fish restaurants along the Bosphorous. He was not alone in offering help initially but Emin had stuck at it unfailingly for all of the three years. He was accustomed to Jeder's rejection that he dispensed on bad days, even when Emin played his trump card, 'Everyone I knew in the military service had a brother or family member who has been killed by the Kurds'. Normally this would be sufficient to engage Jeder in a sombre discussion at least for a few minutes.

This wasn't the moment to deploy that so Emin, detecting Jeder's indifference to the matter belied by an over-confidence that the investigation could have no teeth, reverted to the first mentioned subject. 'These payments....', as he opened a big printout, the contents of which could not be disputed.

Jeder's phone rang and he grabbed the receiver with relish, 'Hello Mehmet'. Emin took this as a signal for him to leave the room taking his huge printout with him. Jeder ruminated on how he was going to spot those intelligent guards with language skills.

'How big is the German export market for Turkish olive oil... via Italy... at the moment?' Mehmet was on the track of labelling. 'Why hadn't you mentioned to me that we could be making official complaints?'

Bulk shipments of extra-virgin oil had been sent to Italy where it was blended with lesser quantities of local oil and marketed as Italian oil and sold on into Germany, and there should have been complaints about trade descriptions on the labelling, but that topic had not been mentioned by Jeder.'Why do I have to find out these things myself?' Each one of his rhetorical questions franked by the unsaid comment 'I can do your job better than you'. Mehmet quickly summarised, 'Please find me the explanations by the morning'.

Emin had hardly left the room and Mehmet had finished the conversation. Jeder sat comatose and motionless in his room gazing into space thinking what he could have done with the money if he hadn't re-directed it.

Whether it was raining or not each day when he left the office building Jeder would walk directly and, as best he could without tripping, in a straight path across the uneven concrete slabs to his car; to leave the premises before anyone could accost him, should they be running after him from the workplace with a piece of incriminating evidence.

It was no different that evening when he started out at 7.30pm. He could have left the office earlier, he didn't really achieve anything by staying an hour later than he had intended. He was putting off the time when he would have to call Gail; he couldn't do this from his office, he had to make the call from home, he certainly did not want to risk anyone overhearing it. He had already put out of his mind the events of the day in the time it took him to cross the bridge in the company Toyota.

His house, situated in a smart residential area on the west side of the Bosphorous, was far too big for his requirements. The real estate agents, instructed by Mehmet when Jeder arrived in the country, had been given a budget predicated on Jeder being married with two children, which was what he had entered on the form requested by the agents. He'd decided to furnish only a couple of rooms - his bedroom, a spare bedroom, a study and the dining room. If guests arrived they would be entertained in the kitchen or else, if it was a more formal event, then the dining room would be used and there were some armchairs and a sofa in his study for relaxation.

There was no one about except a security guard when he reached the compound gates of his villa in Emirgan. The guard waved him through as if this was just another normal day. As he entered the house through the front door he smelt a combination of oil and dampness coming from the enormous basement room which housed the industrial-sized boiler, a huge oil tank, an expansion tank and an unfathomable network of leaking water pipes. The stench crushed his appetite, even though he had eaten only a light canteen lunch of soup and salad seven hours earlier. He put it down to his lack of activity during the afternoon and trying to predict Mehmet's mood the following morning.

He rehearsed several times what he was going to say to Gail, but he couldn't pick up the phone. He looked out of the kitchen window towards his neighbour's house at a child's swing left in the small garden by the previous tenants. His younger son, now aged ten, would have outgrown rocking on that. His sons had never visited, so there had never been a need for an outdoor play area outside his house.

He started picking at food in the fridge, figuring there was insufficient time to prepare dinner, eat it and still call Gail at a reasonable, but not desperate, time. He almost jumped out of his skin when the phone rang. It was Azize. She never called him at home.

'Please report to Mehmet *Bey's* office at 9am tomorrow morning', this was a cordial and respectful request, not a command, as if it was optional, as if there was going to be a reward rather than a reprimand.

Jeder picked up on her unusually relaxed tone 'What is the subject?'

'What do you think?' now she was almost beguiling.

'Ok, I will be there', Jeder suddenly felt tired. His aching feet caused by the long walk the previous day, and now the need to prepare himself for the session with Mehmet the next day, had him deliberating whether to go to bed early without calling Gail. It must have been evident in his voice as Azize cut the call.

Jeder returned to the fridge and sat at the kitchen table, snacking on nuts and fruit, determined to put up any obstacle between himself and calling England. Pacing and sweating, he was unable to call, as if the handset was electrified. Finally and nervously he rang at 10.03pm, 8.03pm UK time. True to form, at the receiving end, after a few rings, the answerphone was triggered into action. Gail's voice reminded him of happier but distant times and he slammed down the phone, only a few words into the message lest she pick up, as he convinced himself that no one was at home and he didn't want to talk. He had done his duty and she could have guessed it was him.

2

FISHES CAN FLY

Nurettin had returned late from Spain on Friday evening to his flat in Nişantaşı. His office had deposited a bulky package inside the apartment front door at the bottom of the stone stairwell. For a few moments as he climbed the stairs to the second floor he wondered why someone from the block couldn't have intercepted the package, opened it and begun to take over his life. Perhaps he was too well respected, or the package was too heavy; he took for granted the honesty of his neighbours.

As he entered his apartment he was greeted by the urgent electronic signal of his answerphone and was glad to drop the parcel abruptly on the wooden floor to give the telephone his full attention. He quickly scrolled down, 'call me back'; 'hello Nurettin, when you receive this, phone me...it doesn't matter how late'; then no message, but just a sigh of exasperation; 'Nurettin, it's Ilker, call me...this weekend'.

He called them in order. Firstly Aruş. 'What is it, Aruş?' playfully, as if anything Aruş lobbed at him Nurettin would fling back twice as hard.

'I'm not doing it anymore'. Even allowing for a poor line, Aruş sounded quiet and distant and gave no warmth to his college friend.

'You're not doing *what*?'

'The payments, you're a cheat'.

'I'm a cheat? I don't think so'.

'I want back everything I've paid you, with interest'.

'You can have it back but why stop now? You are going to be so much richer. There are 35 other people just like you, none of them wants to pull out. You'd be the first. I tell you, it's just starting'.

Aruş cleared his throat. 'I don't want to be involved anymore, I just want what I've already sent you, returned...with interest.' Aruş wasn't talking in a threatening manner but, perversely, Nurettin was slightly concerned that one day Aruş might quietly approach him in the street and gun him down.

'If that's the way you feel about it, you can have it back. But you will be missing out on the proceeds from Ilisu and Yusufeli, which are only a few years away'. How many was a 'few' supposed to be after all? Aruş would have read the papers; he may not have done the research but he might have friends who would have.

'A few years, that's a lifetime for me. Anyway, I don't believe you. How you can possibly have access to any of the sales?'

'You've been following what I have been doing, I have been open all the way'. If Aruş had been there Nurettin would have put his arm around him. Almost immediately though, Nurettin thought more about how indiscreet Aruş could have been. He was the first one to give money and now that Nurettin had other sources perhaps he could afford to be dropped.

'I am very sceptical about the Yusufeli dam project. It's common knowledge that, if and when it is built, the dam would flood 18 towns and villages destroying the homes of around 15,000 people; and, currently, there are no resettlement plans in place for those people'.

'Yes, but the water storage from the dam and the hydroelectric power potential is immense – this is what is attracting western investors. This is why there is so much money floating around this project. It's *all* coming to Turkey.'

'Next week, *my* money, Nurettin', Aruş ended the call. His contribution represented about 10% of the total received but Nurettin had spent it all. Three helicopter rides across central Spain that week still had to be paid for. Nurettin would work out later what he was going to do; first, he needed good news from the other phone messages.

He hesitated a moment before calling Şişko. He wasn't going to be as easy as Aruş.

Then the phone rang.

Nurettin waited to listen to the message. He didn't want to touch the pulsing answerphone for fear of a static shock. He felt hemmed in, standing in the hallway with the phone devices fighting with the coat rack for space. The feeling was amplified by the yellow walls of the long narrow hallway, reminding him that the previous occupants were heavy smokers and he had promised Arzu that he would clean and re-decorate. Arzu's message was short, 'I just wanted to find out how your trip went. I know you're back, unless that's someone else leaving you a message'. From her tone Arzu definitely wanted to talk about something else other than just enquiring about how his trip had gone.

He dialled Şişko. Nobody picked up. He dialled again. Nothing.

He tried Ilker... nothing. 'It would be a real problem if Ilker wanted to pull out; he's the only person as committed as I am, the only other person like me who doesn't mind being constantly rebuffed and belittled', Nurettin muttered to himself.

Then Tunç. 'He has the patience of a gardener', thought Nurettin. Tunç picked up almost instantaneously. 'I have an idea..', Nurettin started. 'I told you not to ring me at home and what is this, 1030 on a Friday night?' Nurettin thought he was about to hang up but Tunç cooled a little from his obnoxious tone. 'It better not be what you told me about a few weeks ago'.

'It's better than that'. Nurettin started as if this was a fresh 9am Monday morning discussion and Tunç had the rest of the day to listen, 'I've started to recruit technical people, water engineers, so we can challenge....even advise...the government functionaries.'

'Look, it's too late in the evening to discuss this, why don't we talk next week?'

'Next week I may have enough people involved, you need to be quick'.

'For this stage perhaps. I'll take my time'. Tunç hung up. At least he wasn't threatening to pull out. Nurettin easily convinced himself not to be despondent. However tenuous was the link to any future return, he still did have friends who believed in him. This was going to be a supine coup. Even if his friends were never going to see any profits they would marvel at his audacity, his persuasiveness and his self-belief. To infiltrate the government, to take money from the government under their noses and be praised by Turkey's foremost industrialist for doing something he thought was unachievable – that will be the reward.

Nurettin gave up with the phone calls and reverted to the package, splitting it open carelessly with scissors, so sure he was that there was nothing of any value inside. He tore the paper which had a string of hand-written messages from his secretary and several documents from the bank to review and sign. Nothing that couldn't be taped back together later. Not all the messages were work related. Three appointments he had asked to be set up had been refused. Firstly, with a low ranking governmental official; he'd acquired this link through a work colleague whose father also worked for the state in Istanbul. Secondly, with a military contact, this was very speculative, Nurettin didn't believe he'd be granted an audience there in a million years. Thirdly, with the head of a regional development bank operating in Eastern Anatolia. There was no degree of rejection from his secretary, no light or shade, as if she too believed this was something that Nurettin shouldn't be doing... so he could hardly expect the answers to be in the affirmative. He'd definitely try all these again. In the previous week, however, he had managed to secure one meeting for the Saturday morning. It was worth switching off now, settling down for some sleep and setting his alarm for 5am. Before he went to bed he erased all the messages on the answerphone.

He was only going to have one shot at this. In the morning he was dropped off by a taxi in front of a wooden villa situated in what he imagined to be a large garden, the whole estate being surrounded by high walls. This must have been, and probably still was, one of the best houses in which to live on the east bank of the Bosphorous.

'Can I help you?,' one of the two security guards was telling Nurettin he'd been dropped off at the wrong place, 'no one comes here, unless you're the President'.

'I'm here to see Mr. Yıldırım. The meeting is at 0930'. The guards couldn't fail to be impressed by his promptness, but weren't accustomed to Mr. Yıldırım entertaining such young-looking people.

'You're a little early. Wait please'. The second security guard went through a pedestrian gate in the large wall whilst the first guard fixed his gaze on Nurettin, defying him to move. The second guard quickly reappeared and nodded.

Nurettin was ushered into a gatehouse inside the wall next to the vehicle access. From there he was just able to catch a glance of part of the garden and a wall of the house. He strained to see more but a third, more senior, guard invited him to take a seat. The chief didn't say it but he meant 'Sit down and be silent'. Two of the three men drank tea, smoked and waited for more than 5 minutes while Nurettin tried to find a comfortable object on which to focus. These physically imposing men formerly guarded some high ranking military person and now they stood in the service of one of the most powerful businessmen in Turkey. Nurettin was, for a moment, intimidated by the bulk of the gatekeepers. He frequently complained to Jeder that he was so much smaller than his brothers but to everyone else he seemed of normal height and in good physical shape.

There were two wall clocks in the guardhouse, the older more elegant one was showing five past nine, the cheaper more modern one was showing the real time, eight minutes past nine in the morning. Nurettin began to stare at the picture of Atatürk on the wall next to the modern clock. This was the black and white portrait that made Atatürk look like a nuclear scientist with his detached starched collar, dark tie, white shirt, dark suit, moustache and unusually, spectacles.

Nurettin's thoughts turned to Arzu who was away in Baghdad, and not due to return until the following Monday. They hadn't spoken for three days before she had left. This was Arzu's way of showing disapproval of the fact Nurettin was trying to meet Tulon to discuss his hare-brained scheme. More likely she was affronted by the manner in which Nurettin had blatantly told her the truth of what he intended to do, in the same way he would explain it to anyone else. His plan was so far-fetched that people might praise him for his boldness, couldn't find the point of the joke or dismissed him as a madman – all three reactions inflating his sense of self-importance. No one stopped him. Perhaps

Arzu had underestimated him, Nurettin thought; she had convinced herself that he would be given short shrift by Hussein Yıldırım. Nurettin concluded that after five years of marriage they still didn't know each other very well. She still hadn't adopted his surname. The things you think but never say.

The telephone in the guardhouse rang and the most senior bodyguard answered. He received the message, 'it's alright, you can bring him through, he has an appointment and he's been checked'. The senior bodyguard nodded to the other two and Nurettin slipped his slim frame nimbly through the guardhouse door in the direction of the garden and ahead of the two security men to try to convey his sense of urgency. The security men were having none of it and commanded Nurettin to wait outside the guardhouse. At least now he had a better view; he was able to admire the garden porticos of the house, the chestnut and fig trees and the cypresses with clematis clinging to the dark foliage. Such was the opulence, and his presence among it, he felt like he was stealing something. These guards would have to frisk him on his way out. Eventually he was shepherded through the garden towards the front entrance to the villa.

The person that Nurettin presumed was Hussein Yıldırım's full-time secretary came to take the baton from the junior security guard outside the front door, shook Nurettin's hand and looked him up and down rather disparagingly, to Nurettin's disappointment. He had deliberated that morning, for several minutes, on the task of choosing the appropriate suit, tie, shirt and shoes. He was led into an impressive marble entrance hall, featuring a cascading fountain directly in front and a double staircase to the side; then through to a salon which featured many beautiful objects from earlier eras, including a Venetian mirror, an Empire console table and some lyre-back chairs. Hussein Yıldırım himself was already ensconced in a much more comfortable-looking modern armchair, sufficiently upright to preserve his formality. He was wearing glasses, reading documents.

Even though it was a Saturday morning, Hussein Yıldırım was dressed in a business suit. He always seemed to be dressed in a suit, he always seemed to be working, whether he was in the office or not. Nurettin admired his work ethic and thought the way to prosperity lay in hard work. Nurettin was glad this business with Yıldırım wasn't related to his bank at all, somehow someone important was going to discuss his water project.

As he saw Nurettin looking around the room at the ancient artefacts, Yıldırım, before formally greeting him, said 'Oh, some of these things came with the house when I bought it a few years ago. I tell people not to touch them in case they might snap.' But Yıldırım did not invite discourse on this subject and quickly moved on, shaking his hand and gesturing Nurettin to sit down in a less grand armchair opposite him.

'You are extremely fortunate to have an interview with me. I know your bank and I know about you from your support to Mehmet, which was much appreciated, but this isn't about your position in the bank'. Yıldırım's welcoming smile and generous jaw immediately set Nurettin at ease, as if he was having tea with a kind uncle. Nurettin checked again to recall that he hadn't stinted on making himself look as serious and presentable as possible and this appeared to find more favour with Yıldırım than it had with his underling.

Nevertheless, Nurettin could already sense this was going to be a very short meeting. He took a folded piece of paper out of his right inside jacket pocket, unfolded it and placed it on top of a real estate magazine with a pen on the coffee table in front of him, 'You don't mind if I take a few notes, do you?'

'It's fine'. Hussein Yıldırım didn't take notes. He memorised what he thought was important and what he could use later. He had someone else, his private secretary, to take notes, maintain his agenda, make certain calls and initiate formal business documents but Yavuz was not required that day.

'At Tulon currently we are favouring investments in water energy. As you know, we have already investments in two heating plants and three small water plants. We are interested in electricity production and eventually electricity distribution. About three-quarters of electricity production is controlled by the state and all the electricity distribution. As you will also know, we are by no means alone with interests and have a watchful eye on this sector.' And, restraining himself for a moment, he qualified that statement with the comment, 'this is all information in the public domain. I'm not telling you anything today other people don't know or could find out by doing a bit of research. But I doubt we will ever focus on just one field of business, so the scale of our investment in this area is, as yet, undetermined.'

Yıldırım continued, 'I can offer you advice on a personal level, but unless you can come to my team with a fully formed proposition then we don't have more to discuss at this time. You will have to take your own decisions, as I am sure you are aware. You need to go away and fully research in which part of the water energy sector it is that you have an interest and what exactly is your point of difference. We have hundreds of these sorts of proposals to evaluate.' Yıldırım relaxed and leant back in his seat and paused.....'by the way, people judge you by the company you keep.'

Nurettin shifted in his armchair; he was going to have to use a trick to keep Yıldırım engaged. His colleagues in the French bank were normally won over by his charm, his politeness, his enthusiasm and his work ethic. He didn't think Yıldırım would be easily charmed.

All the time while Hussein Yıldırım was telling Nurettin what he shouldn't do, Nurettin was thinking about Yıldırım's well publicised comments in the press about how he was indifferent to Turkey's accession to the EU. 'In which particular sectors do you see the Tulon group having geographical expansion opportunities in Syria, Iraq and Ukraine?' Nurettin picked up the folded paper from the coffee table as if he was going to write on it, but this did not deflect his thinking about the company he kept.

'Is this with your French banking hat on?' Yıldırım didn't really expect an answer to that. Nurettin resisted the urge to scratch his scalp as if Jeder was standing there next to him, ready to rib him for it.

'To an extent, government policy leads the way', Yıldırım continued as if he was in a press conference. He wanted to light a cigarette but didn't want Nurettin in his house a moment longer than necessary. 'Each of those countries could be played both sides', he tried to relax as if he *was* smoking a cigarette. 'With extraction and supply of natural resources on the one hand and utilisation of strategic military or commercial bases on the other; all these options would form part of the respective government's negotiations. As a private company, if we chose to go in ahead of government our progress would be stunted'. Nurettin dismissed this as flannel, as he continued to run through all of his associates, how they could be perceived and how Yıldırım knew about them. More to the point, did Yıldırım know everything about him? Perhaps Cengiz, the regional development banker, was toxic, as Nurettin's secretary had suggested; he couldn't keep his mouth shut.

Yıldırım repeated verbatim his company's press statement 'We expect the Iraqi and Syrian markets to take off in the next 10 years. We already have a lot of trade with Russia and we expect great things from Ukraine' but then added, as if it was directly related to what had preceded, 'I am not bothered about successive EU Presidents or factions continuing to find blocking reasons why they say Turkey has not satisfied regulations or conditions required for EU membership.' As Nurettin absorbed this he couldn't help thinking that Yıldırım was stationed in his villa, not living in it. He would sit in this room, have meals in another, and no doubt wash and go to bed somewhere upstairs. This felt like a corporate house; even though he owned it, if Yıldırım wasn't sitting in it then someone similar would be found to replace him. Sibel Doğan, who was at the top of the pile, would see to that. No doubt she already had his succession plan in place. Yıldırım looked like he was approaching retirement date; he was slightly short of wind, a little overweight and possessed a full head of neatly coiffured grey hair. As Nurettin sensed that they would never reach small talk to discuss each other's interests and distractions, Yıldırım gave the impression that he would only be moved from his post when he could no longer breathe.

With an academic air bordering on the professorial, Yıldırım eased himself a little lower in his chair like a man who felt confident his employees were faithfully executing his strategy, such had been the clarity and persuasiveness of his instruction, 'everything our government is doing, and there are a lot of things they are doing right, is setting us on a course to be the leader in this region, and I mean ahead of Iran, because of all the advances we have made on regional inclusiveness. Think of the influence we have from Belgrade to Moscow to Damascus and to Tehran. And we will continue to be more assertive in the region.'

Then, as if, to sign-off but still preaching to an audience bigger than one, 'These rivers are our foreign currency', Yıldırım's phrase made Nurettin feel a little warmer inside as if his grand plan really was the way to go. Then Yıldırım stood up, gradually straightening to ease the stiffness from his back, and gestured to the door indicating he was tired of Nurettin's presence, knowing what he was really there for but with no intention of helping him. Yıldırım opened the door to the hallway, gestured over Nurettin's left shoulder to the housekeeper and carried on talking 'Controlling water flow in our country helps water distribution and improved irrigation. The potential for producing surplus energy and selling electricity to some of our neighbours should not be overlooked'. Then, as the manservant opened the front door of the villa, Yıldırım, making sure he was clearly heard by everyone in earshot, moved impolitely close to Nurettin, and brusquely uttered, 'Is this what you spent your time concocting when we were paying the enormous fees for your bank to save a Tulon company?'

Nurettin left, feeling he had been fleeced of his belongings but determined to create a second chance with Tulon, if not with Yıldırım then with someone else. If Yıldırım hadn't carried out forensic research on Nurettin beforehand, it would only be a matter of minutes before he would be instructing Yavuz to make a few more inquiries. The junior security guard ushered Nurettin from the villa to the guardhouse, cupping his hand under Nurettin's left elbow as if he was a criminal. Nurettin resented this greasy paw touching his freshly dry cleaned suit and sped up to leave his companion trailing.

'I'm wasting my time here, Sibel *Hanım* is the one I need to see', as he moved briskly towards the exit he spoke loud enough in English, half hoping someone would hear. The young guard saw him off the perimeter respectfully enough saying firmly in Turkish that they would sign him out. 'Well, that's that', Nurettin thought to himself, mentally opening his contacts card folder and seeking out the co-ordinates of his next lead.

3

B E B E K   M I R A G E

Arzu stuck out her bottom lip, her spiky black hair protruded over her forehead like spiders' legs or wayward antennae. She had beautiful long, elegant fingers. Her batik print top, in lime, lemon and black, perfectly complemented her dark colouring and hair. She was poised and graceful in everything she did; except that when she turned to face Jeder, she looked constantly indignant, as if he had interrupted her in full flow or had said something about which she was in total disagreement. If she already suspected Jeder was involved in crimes against the state why didn't she say so? She could have told him beforehand he wasn't required, but he was already sitting amongst others in the meeting room when she arrived. Maybe she would find an opportunity to pull him aside during a break or at the end of the meeting. After all, Jeder had never had an opportunity to speak to her directly, except when surrounded by a lot of other people in a meeting room. It had been nine days since the SIU visit, enough time for the whole office to suspect him. Arzu looked at her watch and then directly at Jeder and said 'Let's start.' It was, after all, 8.35am on a Wednesday morning. Two days since she had returned from Baghdad and now back to normality.

He couldn't confirm it, but he was pretty sure he had heard that she was married, probably very happily to a kind and thoughtful man, and she had two children. He thought that she appeared to juggle perfectly the demands of educating the children, keeping house and still she exuded boundless drive and energy. Her business implied she was an advertising executive. In reality she was provided with insufficient funds to run an effective media campaign; but at least she enjoyed a healthy travel allowance. The inferred message from Mehmet was that he doubted the value of expensive TV advertising and preferred she use her time to drum up more export business. Somehow Jeder thought that her extensive absences abroad didn't intrude on the time that her husband and children demanded. All the beautiful women in the office who had introduced Jeder to their husbands had good looking men as spouses; most of them seemed to marry in their twenties and there were no divorces that he had heard about. There was no reason to think the same wouldn't apply to Arzu. The husband presumably took care of the kids when Arzu had to travel to the US, Australia or Baghdad. Maybe she was the principal breadwinner.

Jeder had never met her husband or even seen a picture of him. He just knew he was never going to meet Arzu outside work. But there was no harm in pondering on it for a while. Perhaps she had grown tired of her husband's arrogance which disguised his insecurity and imbalance. It could be that their raised voices, their anger, their screamed arguments, which her husband thought represented drama and conflict, didn't mean passion and love. Maybe the spouse's relentless negativity towards himself made their relationship extremely onerous for Arzu.

There was no way that Jeder was going to tempt Arzu away from her husband. This could not even be for a coffee in a Bebek cafe, a cocktail in an international hotel bar in Beşiktaş or for a fish supper in Sarıyer. No chance to go for a summer evening to sample the view from the Sunset Grill and Bar at Ulus Park. Why, for a moment, would she have wanted to betray her husband and children? Nothing to gain for her, everything to lose.

As for Jeder, just think of the unspeakable damage Arzu's brothers could have wrought on his pathetic body when they arrived unannounced in the middle of the night. Jeder would lie awake thinking about this, after being randomly disturbed in the night, either by a street noise or by the contracting or expanding wood in the fabric of the house; floorboards grumbling ever since unwelcome central heating pipes had been introduced underneath them. These extremes of temperature in the house in the winter causing his piano, caringly transported from England, to be tuned again. There was no one around to play it. Once every two years could not be enough. That's how frequently he thought his boys might visit him.

At the moment when he was expected to be paying attention and was aware that Arzu's glare was about to be locked on him, he imagined himself being decapitated by an animal-headed assassin and then his blood being drunk by Arzu's brothers, her male cousins and her father.

'And we are sure this is the right course of action, aren't we?' Jeder wasn't sure whether she was referring to committing yet more money into the development of an oil blend designed specifically for the US market or these were the instructions being agreed with his killer. Probably both. He nodded hesitantly in Arzu's direction.

This regular Wednesday morning new product development meeting had been due to start early at 8.30. When Jeder had gone first to his office at 7.30 Hakan had not yet arrived. This meeting was scheduled to take most of the morning. At 9.45 Jeder was just on the point of leaving the meeting, eager to make his excuses. He needed to approach Hakan and wanted to try to catch him before he left for his lunch break. Arzu, however, had other ideas.

'Just stay for a few moments please'.

People felt compelled to remain and listen to her out of politeness; the ones that hadn't yet gathered their files to stand up and leave were now caught and Arzu probably thought she could steal five minutes of their time.

She started on the topic of provenance, 'I am proud to have come from Diyarbakır and against many obstacles I have made good in Istanbul,' sounding rather pompous but allowing those born in the provinces to feel that they too had done rather well to be successful in Istanbul. Every time Arzu mentioned Diyarbakır, Jeder thought of Nurettin's scheme and how he might stop it. Here was Jeder's misconception of Nurettin's plan, believing it would affect everyone east of the Bosphorous; but it wouldn't bother people in Anatolia, only the Syrians and Iraqis.

Jeder expected Arzu to make it known that she had a better calling than being a small component in a corporate wheel.

'We all saw on the television last night the report about the girl from Diyarbakır, from my home town', she changed tack, now he thought this was going to be about how her real task was to right the evil wrongs against women in Diyarbakır and Batman.

'I am ashamed about what has gone on there. These were the same type of evil acts you see perpetrated in Stockholm or Stuttgart,' she continued, without any hint of irony.

Inevitably one or two people hadn't seen it, so Arzu eagerly recognised a green light to tell the full story.

Just then the door flew open and Mehmet said, 'This is our room from 10.00'.

'But Mehmet *Bey*', Arzu protested, 'I have it booked until 10.30', as she checked her watch, seeing only 9.48.

With a sarcastic smile that was meant to make everyone feel composed, Mehmet affirmed what was about to happen even if it hadn't been pre-planned, 'I'm sorry, there must have been some misunderstanding, please check with Azize to try to find another available room'.

'But, ten minutes?'

'We need some preparation time', still smiling. Somehow Mehmet's smart 'Sales' suit and tie over-rode the more casual marketing attire of the assembled throng.

'It's alright, I think we were just finishing here', Jeder interjected. Mehmet disappeared to give the all-clear to Azize.

Arzu didn't look at Jeder but gathered her laptop and shoved some loose papers into a carrier bag and made for the exit door. She left her handbag on the table.

As they left the room together and the rest of the participants made a gangway to let them through, Jeder said, 'I stopped you from losing your job'. Jeder had seen the programme. The story was all about chastity and honour and the gruesome killings in their name. The featured girl, was unmarried but then was raped and became pregnant; the unwanted pregnancy started. She tried to flee from her family and her home town. Soon her family caught up with her. A family assembly convened to decide her fate. This consisted of all the male members - her father, uncles, brothers, and male cousins.

'Mehmet doesn't mind my views, I have known him for long enough. I've been to see that girl's pauper's grave in Diyarbakır'. Now they were standing together in the hallway. 'You can imagine the judgement: 'You have brought dishonour to our family. You can no longer live inside our family'', she gestured upwards with her hands and looked up to the ceiling as if throwing up the torn pages of a holy book.

Azize approached from down the hall with preparation materials for Mehmet's meeting and then walked past them into the room. Undeterred, Arzu was now standing at the pulpit carrying on with her homily, reassured that Jeder would not leave. 'Then they made their decision to throw stones at her and slash her with knives. It took that girl seven months to die'. Azize came back out of the meeting room surprised to still see them loitering and, with that look, expected them to move on as they were now dangerously close to Mehmet's space.

'You're talking about that programme last night?' Azize surprised Jeder as if she wanted to join in, but Arzu carried on, 'Some girls' bodies are so tainted that no one from the family is willing to collect the corpse and bury it'. It was dangerous to ignore Azize but Arzu continued to address Jeder. She felt she had to spell it out because he wouldn't have understood the Turkish being spoken. 'Across this very poor region of Turkey from where I come, women are still viewed as the ultimate reservoir of traditional Islamic values'. Now she wanted to be proud of her home town while at the same time being the truth authority.

'Any stain on their honour,' Arzu made sure there was no space for Azize or Jeder to intervene with a comment, 'no matter how inflicted, is automatically punished by killing. Young girls only gain an identity once they are married and bring in generous *başlık*, bride money. So any suggestion of a women being immodest or behaving improperly, or even the rumour of it, throws a shadow over the entire family.' Azize threw both Arzu and Jeder disapproving glances but the diatribe continued unabated. 'The patriarch then knows exactly what he needs to do, and his male relatives are not short of their unthinking support. Once the family has committed the crime, it feels cleansed.'

Once again Jeder was reminded of the animal-headed assassin and people drinking his blood. Then he recalled the live sheep having its throat slit on the pristine floor of the newly opened factory he had visited in Mersin two weeks previously.

Arzu assumed the role of a current affairs teacher, 'the Turkish government's attitude remains extremely traditional concerning women's rights. Families commit honour killings knowing full well that their punishment will be lenient; they will choose a minor to do the deed in the hope of a lighter sentence and then will console the young rogue that when he goes to prison he will be respected and saluted because he has murdered someone in the name of honour. Until recently, there was a law that allowed for leniency in sentencing if it could have been argued that there was 'provocation' (this could be as little as a girl possessing an engaging smile). Fortunately the EU has put our Turkish government under pressure to revoke that law. But although provocation can no longer be cited, extenuating circumstances can and continue to be.'

And then with a despairing smile 'How can you allow a country like this to enter the EU?', Arzu said of her motherland. Maybe she didn't even regard Jeder as male after all. Aware at least that Azize was listening she said quietly to Jeder 'this country still sanctions domestic violence against women and rape in marriage'. Now he knew if he was suddenly transported to London or Manchester with her, it would be easier to ask, but was *she* married?

It would not be inconceivable for Arzu to lose her job over less weighty pronouncements and she wasn't to know whether this would reach Mehmet via Azize. It was definitely not the right time for Jeder to ask anything, especially as Azize's presence accorded a sombre formality to the occasion.

'I've just left a file in there', Jeder sneaked back into the meeting room, making sure the door angle prevented both Arzu and Azize from seeing what he was doing. He went straight over to Arzu's open handbag on the table. Once he'd opened it wide he could see a large purse, a compact, several lipsticks and about ten cardboard packets and a couple of small plastic bottles of pills or loose aluminium strips of pills. 'How many do you need?', he thought. 'Sleeping pills, antihistamines, antidepressants, hay fever, headaches, painkillers, birth control pills?' His woefully weak grasp of the language meant that any large words visible on the packaging weren't helpful and the international brand names he did recognise meant nothing at all in this context. Besides, his own medicine kit consisted of a can of Coke, an apple and a box of alka seltzers. Now he felt the same sensation when as a kid he opened his mother's sewing box for the first time, expecting any minute to be scolded. He initially grabbed a handful of packets, examined each one quickly but then threw the biggest pills, which he thought might be contraceptives, back into the handbag. He stuffed the remaining four packets into his trouser pockets and came back outside to where Arzu and Azize were standing.

He did his best not to look sheepish and put his hands over his bulging pockets and made to leave, as he didn't want to be around when Arzu found her bag.

'Did you find it?' Arzu brought him to attention in the corridor, expecting everything to be properly solved, as both she and Azize and looked at him suspiciously.

'I must have left it somewhere else' was Jeder's unconvincing reply. Before he could start to envisage the situation whereby he could be standing next to her in some English city, she raised her voice again 'there should be no penalty reduction in sentences for murder on the excuse that these are honour killings'. And then smiling to Azize she said, 'and that's the end of the speech for today'. Jeder felt like saying 'You've just lost your job' but Azize's presence precluded that. Azize looked relieved that Arzu had finished before Mehmet came into earshot.

Jeder concluded that this diversion was just one way that Arzu expressed dissatisfaction at the direction her career was headed. Nevertheless, Mehmet had heard the raised voices and as soon as his meeting finished he was keen to meet Arzu and nip in the bud any danger of her losing her job. She was, after all, one of his best employees and he was continually concerned about a headhunter poaching her. While he didn't consider Jeder, or even Azize a problem, he couldn't risk Arzu's loose talk being overheard by another employee. 'Come back to this meeting room at 11', Arzu didn't need to reply to Mehmet as she faced him.

Mehmet smiled confidently at Jeder as he went towards the meeting room 'Just come in here for a few minutes'.

Azize interjected, 'But Mehmet *Bey*, the people are here for your meeting', as she looked at her watch.

'Don't worry, this will only take a few minutes', he said to Azize and then as soon as he entered the room he shouted, 'Someone has left their bag!'.

Jeder sat down awkwardly with his bulging pockets. Arzu came in to retrieve her bag and quickly went out again closing the door firmly behind her. Jeder was happy he didn't have to face her when she next looked inside her bag.

'What you call the Special Investigation Unit..', Mehmet shifted his slim dossier to one side so he could rest his clasped hands on the table in front of him, 'is the department for financial crime. You know there are several units of the Istanbul police force, including smuggling and organised crime. This one for *financial* crime is quite new'. He put a deliberate emphasis on the second time he said the word 'financial' and squinted as if there was something he wanted to spit out of his mouth.

'Is that it?'

'Yes, that's all'. He shouted 'Azize' and the door opened immediately with meeting participants filing in quickly hoping to catch some sport.

As Jeder rose, one of the packets of pills fell from his pocket to the floor behind him. Mehmet saw it immediately almost before Jeder heard it hit the floor.'You've dropped something'. He strained to read the wording as Jeder quickly snapped up the packet.

'Everybody is leaving things behind today', boomed Mehmet, addressing the expectant crowd with his regal smile.... as if he never lost anything. People laughed as if their promotion counted on it.

While Arzu had stealthily disappeared down the back stairs, Jeder strode down the wide hall way to his room at the other end of the floor. He was only vaguely aware of whereabouts she worked even though, in total, the old school building only housed just over one hundred of Mehmet's employees over three floors. He had no idea how and when Arzu arrived at the office each day, whether she drove herself in her own car, her husband or a friend or colleague dropped her off or whether she arrived by *dolmuş*. Now he was more intrigued but not enough to practically do anything about it.

When Jeder reached his office there was no sign of Hakan or Hakan's assistant. Before he had a chance to sit down at his desk Jeder was aware of the presence of someone behind him. Mesut stretched his back, extended one arm and touched the door arch as if to prove he was still growing and that he had as much right to that particular office as Jeder did. In his flawless English, especially for someone who had never been to England, only to New York, 'Jeder, what about the 'Oxel' case?', antagonising Jeder further that he had been eavesdropping on Emin on their discussion earlier in the week.

'Away!' Jeder still didn't fully turn around to acknowledge him and he certainly did not want to invite a facetious comment or further Alec Guinness impressions, whether or not Mesut knew what the 'Oxel case' was. Mesut pretended to be have been thumped in the stomach and disappeared silently with a pained look. What Jeder missed the opportunity to realise was that, for all his irreverence, Mesut had been earmarked and then despatched by the office superiors to convey the message of how disgusted they felt that Jeder had threatened to tarnish the reputation of Mehmet's company, as the news of the SIU raid would have spread like wildfire across the tightly meshed Istanbul business community.

Jeder finally sat down facing the doorway Mesut had just vacated. From a different angle, Azize suddenly brushed past her side door entrance, which was slightly restricted in its movement by untidily hung coats struggling for space with the desk behind the door. Two of the coats were Hakan's even though he wasn't in the office and one belonged to Jeder. As it was still just about summer Jeder was surprised that Hakan hadn't taken these smart winter coats home. Hakan knew they would be secure here, maybe he didn't have room for them at home or perhaps he preferred to regard this office as his real home, it was smarter and someone cleaned it every day. Azize slipped a twice-folded piece of A4 onto the edge of Jeder's desk, quickly made eye contact with him to make sure he had registered that she had left it and then withdrew from the office. It was as if the piece of paper was soiling her fingers; Jeder was sure she was about to go off to the bathroom to clean her hands and wash her face after delivering the wretched thing. Jeder unfolded the paper, which had been handwritten methodically and legibly by Mehmet; the script consisted of a list of demands for information from the Special Investigation Unit. This is what he'd promised when they met eight days ago on the previous Tuesday morning.

'Azize!', he shouted, mimicking Mehmet, which infuriated her, 'do you know where Hakan is?'

He heard the rustling of her skirts as she turned back from Mehmet's room and put her head round the door, 'Hakan is away all week, you remember, he is on a training program', making it clear with her weariness that was the last question she wanted him to ask her that day.

'Another week away after his holiday last week', Jeder complained as Azize disappeared down the corridor. Probably best not to try to contact him there, Jeder thought. And then as if to have the final word, Azize presented herself again 'Mehmet *Bey* will be in Mersin tomorrow', and then quickly left. 'For what? For how long?' Jeder replied not caring whether Azize heard him or not. Jeder could stew in his own juice for a few days.

He started to look closely at Mehmet's note about the Special Investigation Unit's demands, and felt slighted by Mehmet. After all, Jeder was the main actor or at least that was the reaction of his work colleagues. Jeder had spent the uncomfortable half hour with the Unit's staff and Jeder was the person who now had to furnish all the answers and yet he was not allowed to deal with the Special Investigation Unit's staff directly. He could anticipate Mehmet's answer if he was to be challenged on this approach: 'But you don't speak Turkish.....there may be some technical questions that you won't be able to understand so it's better that I talk to them directly myself. I can then re-direct any questions I can't answer to the correct people'. Jeder couldn't deny it as he gazed down the list of demands.

He couldn't dispute Mehmet's superior intellect or negotiating skills. Out of the eight requirements, there were several questions about quality and how Ayvalık checked it; Jeder could only supply answers to two of them himself from his office in Istanbul, for the detailed replies to the other six he would need to contact the Ayvalık office, as these were questions about the quality of olive oil exported over a specific period of months. So Jeder only possessed a quarter of the knowledge required, Hakan would have known more but even he would have had to resort to the Ayvalık office for the details of the particular period in question. At the foot of the page Mehmet had emphasised that, as these answers needed to be available for the Unit by Friday noon, it meant that Mehmet himself would need them on his desk by Friday 9am. There is no doubt Azize had whipped in these instructions as soon as Mehmet had given them to her to provide Jeder with the maximum available time to complete the job.

A day and a half wasn't a realistic time frame in which to gather and present this information, but he knew what the answer would be if he complained. There were just going to have to be some gaps. Azize's mood was the barometer for the office - if she was smiling, life for everybody was going to be easier. Lately, her face bore a terse expression meaning all tasks Mehmet required to be done, in addition to those that she, as Mehmet's agent, requested, would need to be dealt with quickly and concisely.

'Tamer, I need your help', Jeder called the boss of the Ayvalık office. Tamer was the lord of his fiefdom and not someone to be messed with. He really didn't have much time for Jeder, who had only come to visit him once during his contract period which Tamer took as disrespect.

'But it's only Wednesday...you normally call me on a Friday afternoon'.

'I need quality statistics over a 6-month period'.

Each fresh time Jeder called him Tamer expected him to be more deferential, finally he realised this was never going to happen, but at least he was going to have some fun this time, 'And you think I have this in my top drawer?'

'No, but you have someone who does'. Jeder had the impression that Mehmet had already spoken to the people in the Ayvalık office, Tamer didn't ask why Jeder suddenly needed this information.

'Your assistant Hakan has all the statistics that you require'. On this occasion Tamer was particularly cold, distant and rather indignant.

'I need the next level down of detail'.

'I don't know what you do with the data once you receive it in Istanbul, but as far as I am concerned I have nothing to hide, and I can't understand why you would need to change the basic data which we provided to your office, it was the truth after all. I know Hakan has received all the information you need, but I don't know what he does with it after that', referring to Hakan as if he was a third party. 'If there is something specific you require have Hakan call me'. It wasn't the right time to inform Tamer that Hakan does not manipulate the information at all.

'I need quality details....impurities, additives, we don't have that here in Istanbul', there was no way Jeder was going to break up Tamer's formal tone.

'Do you know what you are asking for?'

'I have a long list, free oleic acid levels, steryl glucoside concentrations, polyphenol levels...there's more. How long will this take?'

'Why the hell do they need that?', Tamer paused, although not expecting Jeder to be able to answer. 'Next week....we have a lot going on right now'.

'I need it by tomorrow afternoon'.

'No chance', Tamer remained resolute.

'I need to call you back', Jeder pretended someone had entered his room.

Jeder called back ten minutes later. He could have anticipated that when he did, re-affirming that he needed the information the following day that Tamer wouldn't move from his initial stance.

'I need the information, I know you have it'.

'I thought you weren't going to call back. Don't spoil my entertainment'. Quite what the price Jeder was expected to pay was unclear. Tamer's gruff voice and frequent, considered pauses between sentences re-filling his lungs suggested the owner had the bulk of an Edirne olive oil wrestler, so Jeder was quite surprised when he first met him at a sales conference in Mersin to encounter a small and frail man struggling with emphysema. 'Look....you never meet my deadlines why should I put myself out for you?' Gone was the apparition of Tamer wearing 13kg of leather trousers fitted so tightly that his opponent was unable to grip to make a meaningful move. The actual vision of vulnerability encouraged Jeder to persist with increased supplication on each subsequent call.

He just needed to keep the conversation with Tamer going as he couldn't be sure if Hakan would back him up. 'Ask....Mehmet to call me', was the progress Jeder had made by the fourth call. This was going to push Jeder right up to the deadline. He couldn't afford to leave for home without having secured some commitment. He began to contemplate Mehmet's reaction on Friday morning after reviewing Jeder's proposed replies. Then Tamer put down the phone.

4

ANATOLIAN FAULT

Saturday morning at 5am Nurettin was disturbed in his sleep as the phone rang and diverted to message. He was sufficiently awake to hear the same demand from Aruş that he had delivered every day that week.

'One day that's going to be your mother calling', Arzu complained as she rolled away taking the sheet with her. Nurettin went to the kitchen to find his case, which contained his diary. The hall was a no go area and the phone a contaminated piece of equipment. He'd forgotten that he'd agreed to have lunch with Jeder at a restaurant in Bebek. Nurettin had chosen one partly for its speed of service recognising that, like him, everyone eating there needed to be in and out quickly; but primarily because the restaurant served his favourite casserole, a lamb and quince stew popular in western Anatolia.

He arrived before Jeder and elected to sit indoors in the old-fashioned dining room away from the sun's intrusion rather than on the terrace.

Jeder recognised his black curly hair, his slim frame, neatly pressed trousers and casual figure-hugging shirt from the rear. Nurettin was chatting to the restaurant owner. He turned to face Jeder.

'Let's sit down', agreeing with the restaurant owner to take the last small table overlooking the Bosphorous. Nurettin struggled to wedge himself into the seat, compromised by another table and chair behind him. 'At least there is one benefit from being so small', he always complained to Jeder that he was so much smaller than his brothers, but to everyone else he was normal height. Nurettin was one of five brothers born and raised near Izmir. Nurettin's brothers were all more naturally gifted than he, whether with their school work or at basketball and football. He so wanted to be as talented and skilful as them. Try as he might, Nurettin never quite achieved their marks or distinctions or praise in class. On the basketball court or soccer field he never stood out like they did. He was never going to catch the eye of the Karşıyaka or Altay youth coaches. He had never liked volleyball. He was the runt of the family, at least three inches shorter than the smallest of his brothers. Now at 29, he was living and working in Istanbul after muddling his way through his studies at school and fortunately achieving a place at the Boğaziçi Üniversitesi, reading geology as his first degree and staying on to do his masters in water collection, distribution and consumption, performing reasonably well there and really impressing in job interviews thereafter. Now he was the most priapic of all his brothers. His burgeoning self confidence was not totally based on his physical appearance. He was obsessive in his neatness, both in his appearance and his actions.

'So, what's it all about, why the urgency? You go to your boss when you feel threatened but you come to me when you seek an opportunity, right?' Although it was a Saturday Nurettin treated it like a workday, lunch had to be short. 'I've already ordered for us, by the way'.

'You always said that if I was going to be involved with the government ministries then I should let you know', Jeder had a chance to say something, aware that a waiter was already bringing their starters.

'No. What I told you about a year ago was *don't* arise the suspicion of the Turkish governmental agencies, you will find some very bright and highly educated people there', Nurettin gestured to the waiter to hold back.

'How have you *now* become involved, it's always been difficult for you *not* to be involved? People in the government processed your work permit, granted you security clearance. You are already on the radar screen of a mid-ranking civil servant.' Nurettin asked the waiter to come.

'Your name is a file. In that respect you are not so unusual or different to any other foreigner living here', a dish of *cılbır* was placed in front of him while the restaurant owner gave Jeder *hamsi sarması*. In no time Nurettin had swallowed the first poached egg whole.

'It's a little more involved than that, I will have to attend a court hearing', Jeder was not eating his anchovies yet as if he needed all his attention and demanded Nurettin's focus on this matter.

'What's the subject?', Nurettin continued eating with the same intensity that he expected information.

'Price fixing, probably', Jeder hoped this might slow down Nurettin's consumption.

'And for whose advantage is that meant to be? Up or down? Do they want the Americans........?' appearing to be paying a little more interest in what Jeder was about to say.

'Or the Germans', Jeder interjected. He could have talked about the HDE article if only Nurettin was not so pressed. In a meeting earlier that week Mehmet had surprised Jeder by producing an article from the *Lebensmittel Zeitung* with a Turkish translation already done by an outside agency. The story read 'The German Federal Government is attempting to push through a ban on selling products below the acquisition price and this ban targets primarily foodstuffs. The reason for this is the ruinous fierce competition among retailers. Trade associations will have the opportunity to comment on the draft.' Mehmet had picked up the phone to call Eckhard Weitz, Director of the German retailers' association *Hauptverband des Deutschen Einzelhandels* (HDE), directly to discuss the matter in English. Mehmet despised the protectionism through EU subsidies that were offered to its own members, restricting direct access of Turkish products to European markets. He told Weitz that the German Federal Government risked completely excluding Turkish products from the German consumers, and that would be very unpopular in large parts of the country. Weitz shrugged off that comment but warned that a total ban may lead to price control and hamper business for retailers. 'You see', Mehmet concluded to Jeder, 'how quickly our markets can be closed'. Mehmet didn't need to say he was referring to the Ozel case.

'The Americans or the Germans, do they want them to pay more or less?' Nurettin continued, almost completely through his starter, 'you don't sell much to the Turkish market do you? So you can't be the main culprit?' he tried to dilute Jeder's anxiety, which he sensed from the fact that he hadn't started eating. Nurettin had completely finished his starter, leaving no trace of yogurt or egg on his plate or on his lips.

'It has been like this for some time, but now there is more focus. Generally all the producers are making money in a business where margins traditionally have been very poor. When source prices have gone up we have passed it on. When source prices dropped we didn't reduce retail prices so much. You either take big risks and periodically fall on your face, or you make no money. It's not clear who has raised the alarm, possibly some of our disgruntled customers...the big retailers'.

'Or perhaps the government found out about it, itself. And.... *have* you been fixing the prices?', Nurettin wiped his face with his napkin, although there was nothing to remove. Looking at Jeder's vine leaves, 'If you and all the other trading companies are in this together you can all share the fines. Olive oil is a glamour export, the government is not going to scald the industry, is it?'

'You know it's not that simple', Jeder was beginning to become a little agitated. Nurettin was loud and there were other tables in earshot. Jeder now hoped that brief replies would extinguish Nurettin's curiosity, after all he had never previously been that interested in the details of what Jeder had been doing.

Jeder felt compelled to provide Nurettin with some background, to at least let him form his own judgement, on what the investigation might be about, 'They searched through all the papers in my office', he started a little more earnestly but was aware how farcical it looked as he beckoned Nurettin closer so he didn't need to raise his voice.

'They didn't ask to see any computer files. Mehmet had advised me ages ago that if ever we experienced such a visit the best tactic was that I should stay in my office all day, just sitting at my desk, and let them fuss around me as they would not feel comfortable in my office. In actual fact they made me feel like the trespasser, that these papers belonged to the investigators or at least they were Turkish government property and nothing to do with Mehmet's company', Jeder cut through one of the vine leaves and tasted a piece of fish. 'On the one hand, they took away many report documents in English but they left the computer. I heard later that they had been to the IS department and had taken some back-up files, the wrong ones, but they wanted me to be aware that they knew most of the sensitive information was stored on computer not on hard copy.'

'This all sounds a little pedestrian and not the SIU that I had heard about, no?', Nurettin started chewing hard on a slightly stale piece of bread as if it was tobacco.

'I think they were looking for any documents that generated taxable transactions; third party company names and individuals who had provided and delivered goods; plus, of course, all cross-border transactions, these were the ones most likely approved by me. They wanted to interview Mehmet about these transactions.' Jeder started eating in tiny mouthfuls, so that he could continue talking while Nurettin began fidgeting with side plates and unused cutlery, 'there were many actions, particularly involving the border countries, commissions, duties, subventions and discounts surrounding export sales, about which I did not always have all the information. Other than from where the money was paid or to which bank the remittance was sent, at least in the first instance – it wasn't clear what they were going to do here. The rules surrounding the commission and rebate structure were myriad, designed to keep government duty auditors in gainful employment.'

'Well, I thought most procurement fraud is uncomplicated and should be easily detected?', Nurettin stood up to try to attract any waiter's attention, 'I guess it's happening all the time, but the minority of companies who actually know about it are also the ones who are reluctant to display their dirty clothes in public, so everything's OK, isn't it, it's not going to change?'

Nurettin didn't really see any exposure for Jeder. It was very unlikely he was going to make any significant personal gain through his day job. Otherwise why involve himself in Nurettin's scheme? Unlike Aruş and Şişko he wasn't going to ask for the money back, it was never his.

Nurettin sat down again as he saw a waiter on his way with the main course, 'I can't remember the last time I went to the mosque'. He turned away from watching Jeder still eating his starter to look out over the waterway in the direction of the opening to the Black Sea, 'Before university....in Izmir...with my father'. This was consistent with his behaviour to be awkwardly dismissive of his devout compatriots and look down on any of his colleagues who sent their children to religious schools.

The waiter held back until Nurettin had finished speaking and Jeder eating before he cleared the starter plates.

Nurettin was far more interested in the strategic importance of Turkey as a water super power. With the Nile, the Amazon and the Danube all at risk, water was the strategic issue. Climate was forecasted to become an economic nuisance as storms, droughts and hot spells would create havoc for farmers, who would then have to resort to desperate measures in order to irrigate their fields; consumers trying to cope with a worsening scenario of spiralling food prices and a lack of drinkable water and, if they could ever afford them in the first place, higher insurance premiums due to the resultant property loss and damage.

'It's not difficult to imagine vast numbers of migrants trying to come to land-locked Europe; after being forced from their own land, saturated and ruined by the rising of sea levels or, on the other side, without any water to be able to grow crops.'

Nurettin hesitated as the waiter brought large dishes of *kuzu ve ayva yahnisi* and waited until he was out of earshot before continuing.

'Turkey holds a great strategic position. It already controls the taps on Syria. Now with the deal with Israel on supplying tankers of water from another major water source, the country can further cement that alliance in return for arms. This move will further frustrate the Arab nations in the Middle East. It will also show the EU and the US that Turkey can do deals independently in the region, all those vociferous liberals will have trouble attacking it'. Nurettin started his lamb casserole as if it was his last meal.

'Yes, but that won't stop Turkey being criticised on Northern Cyprus and the Kurds'. Jeder wasn't ready to start his main course and was increasingly conscious of the people on the table behind Nurettin listening to their conversation.

'Where the Northern Cyprus issue is holding us up is the delay to the entry to the EU; we're missing out on all those subsidies for agriculture and transport and major power projects. Not to mention money for infrastructure planning projects, putting land to more politically productive use, attracting investment and jobs from international inward investment', Nurettin was already half way through his plate, despite almost talking continuously. 'Until that EU pot of gold arrives, Turkey is going to have to continue to rely on the endless IMF loans and the erratic income from tourism. Every second year people outside see internal bombings or international terrorism incidents here or in Ankara. I'm thinking about the shopping mall bomb in 1999'.

Nurettin had told Jeder that he had a girlfriend, he had a smart flat in the upmarket district of Etiler, and he was working for one of the big French banks. This last statement Jeder knew to be fact, the previous two he could not verify. Despite the fact that they had spent late nights working together during the economic crisis there had never been an occasion when Jeder needed to answer the phone on Nurettin's behalf to speak to his girlfriend. It wasn't so unusual that Nurettin had never invited Jeder to his flat, they always ate out; wherever Nurettin chose the food it was generally excellent and inexpensive. Jeder understood Nurettin's girlfriend had a job that involved a lot of travel, so she wasn't usually there in Istanbul at the weekends. Jeder had stopped enquiring about her as Nurettin volunteered less and less information.

Nurettin said he regularly travelled abroad on business and occasionally for pleasure. He spoke English fluently, French very well, was very keen to learn more Spanish, but didn't know enough Spanish speakers in Istanbul or multi-lingual French work colleagues in Paris with whom he could practice. Although his father never lived long enough to see it, Nurettin had now already achieved much more than any of his brothers. Most of the time, especially when surrounded by family members and work colleagues in Istanbul, he was bristling with confidence. Beyond those circles he was careful not to appear arrogant or offend anyone's sensibilities. But inside, in fact now, he felt he could do just about anything.

'We need to spread out those repayments to the IMF more evenly', Nurettin finished his stew. 'We don't want to risk inflation spiralling out of control again like it did in 2001 and during the decade before. We are looking at billions of dollars here. And by the way', he continued, 'while the US is stupid enough to think that Turkey can be a model for Washington style democratisation and a firewall to terrorism from the East, then we will have their money and technology as well!'.

'You have to concede on Cyprus first', Jeder had finally caught up with the meal.

'Concede, why should we concede? That's what the Europeans want us to do. Why should we give way on Northern Cyprus? Most Turkish people want support for Denktaş. Why should we withdraw Turkish troops from the island, the territory is ours? Recolonising the Greek Cypriots into the North of the island is reminding us of the terrible implications of the mistakes that were made over the population exchanges between Turkey and the Greeks in the 1920s, it never worked. The Greeks wouldn't want to come into Turkey, nor would Turks want to live in Greece now. The proposal is flawed.' As he said this, Nurettin felt a tinge of sadness although he did not show it to Jeder. He recalled once at a family dinner in the suburb of Üçkuyular that his father had said how lucky they all were to be living in Izmir, but how the city had deteriorated and faded from the cosmopolitan melting pot his grandfather had described. 'We are Turks', Murat, one of Nurettin's elder brothers had proudly shouted. Nurettin's father looked on disapprovingly, but nobody was sure whether it was for Murat being so raucous or what it was he had said.

Then, for their dessert Nurettin had requested small bowls of *kuru incir receli*, a fig jam, which they ate with teaspoons together with traditional sherbets and more water.

'We will wait for Iraq to see what they will do before we make any decision on the Kurds,' Nurettin began to tenuously relate the situation of Greeks and Armenians in Izmir in 1922 before the secular republic was established in Turkey to the Kurds in South-East Turkey in 2002. 'Why not take in the whole of the Caucasus', he thought. It was his regular obligation to give the rather uneducated Jeder a history lesson. 'The PKK is still there. My brothers and my cousins have the scars to show for it and some of my friends are dead. I cannot forget that and I am not sure I can ever forgive in my lifetime. I am worried about what the Americans and the British will propose for Iraq. They don't really understand it, not like they think they understand, but don't dare to solve, the Israel and Palestine issues. I can't see the Americans putting pressure on the PKK to disarm or demobilise. This is just talk.'

'Of course the US will give something in return to the Kurds', Jeder said.

'Although they fought against Iraq, they will not be given Kirkuk or the oil'.

'For Kirkuk to change hands would send the whole region to hell', Nurettin agreed.

'Everything depends on the Americans', Jeder was referring to the fact that Turkey was dependent on IMF loans, the renewal and renegotiation process around which was always dependent on the Americans. Which is why it was so surprising that the Turkish parliament would vote against allowing US troops to be stationed in Turkey. The US were still smarting from the rebuff which prevented them from stationing up to 60,000 troops in South Eastern Turkey at the border, to keep order in Northern Iraq. There was sure to be a consequence, 'If Washington gives the green light, then the Kurds can go ahead and take Kirkuk and do as they please,' Jeder said.

Nurettin stopped smiling, stood up and tossed Jeder's suggestion into the bucket. 'Turkish soldiers in Iraq then would come face to face with the American military... it is most unlikely the US would let this happen'. One of the waiters came over to see why Nurettin was standing up. Nurettin asked for another jug of water, which arrived promptly.

He poured himself another glass of water and sat down again, 'If the Americans want to maintain their relationship with Turkey they must be very cautious with their approach'.

He could have puffed his chest out. He conveniently blocked out what he had heard the Kurds were saying but he thought he would say it anyway – 'Kurds are only wanted (by the US) for dirty work; they will have to back off from Kirkuk because Turkey has undue influence with the US, thousands of Kurds in exile are prepared to go back and live or die in Kirkuk; Kurds will not retreat from the strategically most important city in *Kurdistan* ; stay in Kirkuk, Kurds, fortify all strategic positions, don't sell your honour, your dignity, your past history, your past struggles'.

He took another sip of water, stood up and started to walk around as if he owned the place. He found a waiter and asked for the bill and then returned to the table taking the serviette to wipe his mouth.

'There is no plan for such a thing that might be called Kurdistan', he concluded as he sat down again, 'Let's wait for Iraq until after 2005, there is no hurry,' he smiled, confident that Turkey held several aces.

Understandably, most Western European spokespersons were saying that it was clear that the EU polls had it right, the EU states electorate were correct to be cautious about Turkey's impending candidature.

'Back to Europe', Jeder said, now unsure whether the meal had emphatically finished or was going to continue with the waiter bringing *mignardises*. '80% of the EU electorate does not want Turkey in the EU' 'You recall those posters under the bridge on the way from Orly to Porte de Sevres, *'Turquie plus Constitution – NON ! – Je garde la France'*. Then the waiter arrived and planted a small box in front of Nurettin on the table.

'Yes but,' Nurettin countered, '75% of Turkey wants to join the EU. Turkey is also a key NATO ally at the intersection of the Balkans, the Middle East and the Caucasus.'

He then rocked back in his chair and smiled, 'but then.......one third of Turks believe that suicide attacks against Americans and other westerners belonging to occupying forces in the Middle East are justified'.

'So we have a stalemate'.

'No, we have the US on one hand and the EU governments, <u>not</u> the EU electorate, I stress, on the other. Who do you think will win?' Before allowing Jeder time to assess the question, let alone formulate the answer, Nurettin carried on 'the Germans go to Antalya for their holidays, first class hotels, lovely beaches, water sports, beautiful scenery, golf courses, good weather in July and August and cheap … for them. What do their foreign ministers know?'

'I think the Italians and the French will be a little more cautious', Jeder said, 'when considering the supposed secularity of the state, even if they only visit Istanbul, they still see all the head scarves and *gecekondular* full of migrants from the east, why stop at the Bosphorous? They also look at the numbers, they recoil in their chairs when they see the figure of 25 million Anatolian farmers. Remember still in France the importance of the agricultural lobby'.

'I think the French are more worried about whether we have a sound judicial system and whether corruption in business is a thing of the past or not', Nurettin rose again, this time throwing down his serviette, picking up the box and pushing his chair fully back under the table. When the Italians and the French were mentioned in the same sentence, Nurettin remembered his father's family stories about how the French and Italian ships, together with those from Britain and the USA, anchored in Izmir port in 1922, refused to allow asylum to any of a quarter of a million refugees, as three-quarters of the city was burned to the ground. His thoughts became momentarily muddled, so it was a good time to leave the restaurant.

'Next time I will take you for dinner at Tike in Levent', said Jeder, trying to attract Nurettin's attention and stretching for an excuse to justify a visit to his favourite restaurant. Nurettin appeared to ignore him and went over to settle the bill and for a brief chat with the manager, not intending Jeder to be part of the conversation.

As they moved towards the exit, Jeder was still trying to construct his answer to the earlier comment about attacks on western occupying forces in the Middle East, with the Western media seemingly biased towards the emphasis on identifying and reporting suicide bombings. 'Suicide bombers or suicide blasts were today launched against occupying forces and buildings. Security was breached but has now been re-established', was the familiar headline reporting, instead of 'attacks by militants or insurgents'. Somehow this made Jeder think that European governments would never be able to persuade the majority of Europe's electorate to change the myth that Western governments are doomed to perennial conflict with Islam. But for Nurettin this conversation was closed.

Nurettin had the objective of thinking he could construct an elaborate scheme to control the water supply to Syria, so that he can extort profits from the Turkish government. At one point he was thinking he could become a supplier alongside the government, but set high cartel rates for the customers. But he had not yet found anyone close or within government who would listen to his plot and how now he was going to hold the Turkish government to ransom was certainly unclear to Jeder. At face value Jeder's involvement was limited, he was supplying small amounts of money to Nurettin who would use that for lobbying business leaders; this group was slowly replacing members of the military as the presiding influence over the government. 'Think of it as a low risk investment with a massive coupon!' was Nurettin's chant that Jeder remembered each time he sweated when the subject of commission payments was mentioned by anyone in the Üsküsdar office. How quickly that dividend would materialise and in what form, or in which country Jeder would receive the money was less clear, but Nurettin's recent pronouncements had indicated that it would be east of Turkey rather than west. Jeder was never going home.

It was raining as they spilled out into the street.

'What about Spain', Jeder asked.

'Next time', Nurettin pointed to his watch.

5

FLOAT DOWNSTREAM

Javier had the appearance of someone who had something much more important to do later. Nobody looked as smart as he did when they took their dog for a walk. He was not taking his dog for a walk on any ordinary sidewalk. This was one of the most prestigious streets of Salamanca. In fact, only a two minute walk from the Retiro Park.

There was some promise in the meeting with Nurettin. Javier had never met anyone from Turkey before but his friend, Mario, assured him that it would be worthwhile. In the resulting telephone conversation, Nurettin was polite and sounded genuinely interested in Javier's expertise and background.

Javier tried to manoeuvre his dog at the end of the lead past an elderly couple on their constitutional. The man, in his late seventies, but who looked much older as a troublesome hip slowed his walk to an uneven shuffle, was wearing some natty khaki shorts and smart brogues, a healthy bronzed visage, with economies of well-groomed grey hair. The dog lead caught the man's right ankle to make his leg rise, putting an uncomfortable strain on his other leg, which almost succeeded in bringing the couple down, as his wife gripped ever harder on the old man's forearm. Javier was on the point of lending some stability to the situation, but thought that physical contact would not be appreciated by the couple unless they could not manage by themselves. They would have to be certain to fall for it to be correct for Javier to intervene. After all he was only thinking how awful it would be if one of them fell and broke something at their age, surely to avoid this event, rules of etiquette could be partly disobeyed. In the event, it was a bench itself that provided the necessary prop for the lady, who surprised Javier with her ability to support her unbalanced husband while at the same time not doing herself any damage on her heavy contact with the wooden seat.

This was the sidewalk bench where Javier had pre-arranged to meet Nurettin at 11.30 that morning. So, as Javier loitered, and the elderly couple took time to compose and readjust themselves, they thought he must be courteously holding back to look after their welfare and was making sure all was well before they could continue. After a minute or so, they acknowledged his kindness and carried on.

Five minutes later, Javier spotted Nurettin in the distance, arriving on a bicycle. Nurettin looked slim and healthy, even though he said he had no interest in going to the gym. Once Nurettin had propped up his bike against a Mimosa tree and sat down, Javier started, 'in 25 years, huge parts of Spain will be desert. The causes we are both very familiar with – irresponsible land use, global warming and soil erosion', Javier mimicked Nurettin's lecturing style from their telephone conversation. 'Almost a third of the Spanish mainland is currently affected by desertification where farming, construction and other activities combined with rising temperatures, are causing plant life to retreat, giving way to land that would be lifeless without human intervention', he continued.

'Of which there is too little', Nurettin added.

'Can you imagine half of Andalusia turning to desert', said Javier.

Nurettin recalled the vast grain fields on his first visit there. 'The point is that actually two-thirds of the whole country could be described as arid, semi-arid or dry sub-humid – there are entire areas prone to desertification. The quality of the water in these areas is very bad, very salty, which in turn is leading to desertification'.

'You've read the UN report, I suppose, which warns that 40% of the global land mass is at risk and 1.2 billion people', asked Javier.

'Do you believe it?'

'I know that in Spain we signed up those UN objectives back in '96 but we've never enacted them'.

Nurettin recalled the banner headlines 'Combined International Effort Required to Check Desertification' and thought about how the Turkish government could increase the flows of the Tigris and the Euphrates and how positively this would be received as an equitable sharing and co-operation. After all, there was still no universal treaty in force to regulate the use and protection of shared waters. It had taken many years to prepare the Law of the Non-navigational Uses of International Watercourses and after its adoption by the UN General Assembly in 1997 only 16 states had subsequently ratified it. The legally binding obligation was not necessary when there was a trade-off, between providing increased food and energy production in return for eventual economic integration and enhanced co-operation on a broader scale.

'When the Iznajar dam was built all those years ago do you know how many homes they had to move?'

'I think about 500 homes, maybe 2,000 people. Why are you so interested in this one?'

'It's big. There's a good ratio between how many people were displaced and how many people have guaranteed water supply because of the dam, about 200,000, I believe'.

Over the last two years Nurettin had been travelling to Spain as much as possible on weekend breaks, fascinated by the similarities with Turkey, at least as far as drought and water control were concerned. That year in Spain, for weeks before the tourist season starts, swimming pools had been empty, city fountains turned off and golf courses ordered to reduce watering. Reservoirs in the south-east were more than three-quarters empty; regions were forced to restrict the use of re-cycled water. Crops had been left to wither as irrigation for agriculture, which accounted for three-quarters of Spain's water, had been heavily restricted in order to save water for domestic use. Previous programmes to divert water from the northern rivers such as the Ebro to the parched south-east, had long been shelved. Diversion was going to be Nurettin's particular interest. Environmentalists who were opposed to diverting water from the north, had complained that desalination was not the best solution and, of course, wanted restrictions on building for tourism in the south–east, which was mainly to satisfy a British, Dutch and German demand. Spain's green north-west areas had abundant water supplies and the Costas in the South were not expected to suffer problems.

Nurettin had even reminded Jeder about potential drought problems as far north as Britain 'You're talking about desalination plants off the coast of Spain, but with the population growth in your little island, it won't be long before you will need a desalination plant in the River Thames.'

'What about Portugal?', Nurettin wanted Javier to talk about it the neighbour in the Iberian peninsula, dependent in part from transfer of water stocks from Spain. Not only were there regional disputes within Spain and conflicts between farmers and cities, there was already a brewing national altercation between the Spain and Portugal.

'Well, Portugal is filing a claim', began Javier, 'as Spain has turned the taps off on the flow of water from the Duero, which runs from eastern Castilla y Leon and empties in the Atlantic in Northern Portugal. The Spanish argued that 50 per cent less rain has fallen since the same time period a year ago, making conditions the driest Spain has endured since the National Meteorological Institute began collecting rainfall information in 1947. Portugal was claiming compensation of €6 million which the Spanish Environment Ministry was most likely to pay'.

'Why's that?'

'Well….', Javier turned his head slowly towards Nurettin. One side of his mouth lifted slightly, creases formed to the side of both his eyes, but the smile that should have followed didn't. Nurettin noted the ginger as well as the grey streaks of hair around Javier's temples. 'What is a €6 million fine compared to the €82 million programme which will be running from 2005 to 2008, required to combat desertification in Spain?'

Javier had recently emerged from a trial accusing him and his water company of allowing potentially dangerous levels of a herbicide to form in the largest reservoir in the region of Cordoba and Malaga. Around 200,000 people had been forced to drink only bottled water and any water they could obtain from specially provided but insufficient street corner bowsers. Water inspectors had been called in after an inside tip-off and discovered double the permitted level of the chemical terbuthylazine in the water of the Iznajar reservoir. This herbicide is used to kill weeds but what the authorities were most interested in was how such a high concentration could have been allowed to enter the water supply. As ever, Javier's company was caught between the restrictions of flexibility of source options, constrained by the impact of the worst drought in Spain for 60 years, and the demand for his public water company to make a profit. Javier delayed the purchase of active carbon, the remedy required to reduce the chemical concentration. When he eventually sanctioned the purchase he only ordered 2,000 kilos, a quarter of the required amount.

Javier said in court, 'It was not my responsibility to test the levels of herbicide in the Iznajar reservoir. It was not my responsibility to order the active carbon. It was not my responsibility to resign. It was my responsibility to inform the public, which is what I did. I will not be a scapegoat. I should be exonerated.' Unfortunately, two people had died; the chemical having proved fatal when consumed in high concentrate over a long period of time. He hoped that the two court cases, filed by the relatives of the two people who died, would be rejected by the Spanish courts; they needed to find that there was no direct relationship between his lethargy to take the required safety precautions and the accidents which resulted in the deaths.

He had tendered his resignation two days after the action was filed but his director, under the orders of the Interior Minister, had rejected it and told Javier to carry on with his job.

'You said you were going to offer me a contract?'

'It won't look like the contract you had with your water company. Think of it as a payment for lobbying and information'.

Javier had another option, to ingratiate himself with the contractors involved in upcoming major infrastructure projects. The Spanish government had secured Kuwaiti money to build massive desalination plants, capable of producing 10,000 cubic meters of water per day. These were beginning to spring up all over the North-Eastern Spanish coast. Major projects to harvest rainwater were also being put in place. But right now, after his dealings with government, it seemed easier and potentially more rewarding to side with Nurettin even though he had never travelled further east than Sicily.

'What's this about?'

'Well, Aleppo depends entirely on water from the Euphrates for its residents. Same with Salamiyah. The respective governments are a long way off addressing the issue of Turkey's rapid economic development and its consequent demand for water resources'. As Nurettin said this, he still had in the back of his mind that he hadn't convinced Tulon. 'Javier, I'll leave it with you'.

He expected to be contacted by Tulon by phone in Spain at any time or over the weekend back in Istanbul.

Nurettin met with Mario for a late lunch in the Plaza de Santa Ana.

'How was it with Javier? I guess he told you all about Iznajar?'

'He did. I'm not surprised he left', Nurettin had no intention to discuss anything more about Javier with Mario. 'You know, I'm glad to exchange my Istanbul rain for your Spanish sunshine'.

'Well, I've just come back from 2 days in central Spain, in the helicopter, monitoring water abuse. It was hot there. It's frustrating, the guys there never have sufficient resources to carry out what's required on surveillance. There will soon be a war brewing between Castilla-La Mancha and Murcia.'

Mario's company was importing and selling US-made satellite equipment to the Spanish authorities, so he was quite often in the air demonstrating or extolling its virtues. Murcia, was full of fruit groves and golf courses, so Castilla-La Mancha was reluctant to accede to the local government's demands of 120 hectometres of water from its reservoirs, and stuck quite resolutely to its offer of 30 hectometres. Mario believed this was just desserts for an area that, along with Valencia and Andalucía, targeted golfers from the UK and Ireland with up-market residential and tourism complexes built around top class courses.

'*Señor*, the golf courses started out by escaping the restrictions on property developments,' Mario didn't really like golf nor golfing people.

'It doesn't matter, the spaces that are being taken are deserted spaces and not productive arable land, I don't see any rain forests being destroyed, who cares?' Nurettin displayed an indifference bordering on rudeness towards his host.

'Golf is a real estate activity, to sell property, to find different routes to comply with building regulations. Some of these projects can start before there is any environmental assessment.'

'There is no threat to food security!', Nurettin looked around him from his pavement table. He was beginning to enjoy the afternoon atmosphere in the square and, by sitting outside, he was in the thick of it. The noisy girls shouting loudly at the boys. Freely available drink and different types of smoke contributing to the noise levels. People convening generally for a hedonistic experience. No sign of police reining this in.

'Farmers dig more wells drawing on the same stressed source...and then, when those groundwater levels are depleted, they just dig deeper wells', Mario could see his country evaporating as his satellite measurements revealed the staggering loss of groundwater over the past few years.

'So where are the major imbalances of water stocks across the different regions here?'

'Northern Spain's water basins are well stocked while Segura and Jucar, serving the south and south-east of the country are barely a quarter full. Levels in the Entrepeñas reservoir in Guadalajara are now at a record low'.

'So, it's a money and politics game?'

'Also, water saving is a factor. Or the lack of it. It's a bit like the EU. Municipalities know the water saving measures, but who is there to enforce them? Murcia has the money but not the political backing to support major water transfers essential for their livelihood. Murcia is pumping vast quantities from elsewhere in Spain from underground aquifers. Twenty-five years ago it was one of Spain's poorest areas. In 1979 a canal was dug to allow millions of cubic metres of water to be imported from the Tagus river basin and this stimulated one of the greatest explosions of intensive farming in Europe. More than 100,000 hectares are now being farmed under plastic, mostly supplying British and German supermarkets.'

'So now, if the water supply was cut off, the local economy in Murcia implodes. No more water melons, broccoli, celery and tomatoes'.

'Well, fewer. Smaller and poorer quality, I suppose.'

'Then their food production industry dies as they can no longer meet the demanding standards of the British and German supermarkets'.

Mario continued, 'At the start of every drought period people are panicked into thinking that the latest drought could be much worse than the last one they can remember. We both know these figures. We consume 5 litres of water a day. If we include washing, bathing and other essential functions, somebody in Western Europe could use up to 150 litres per day. And if we include swimming pools, suburban lawn sprinklers and various outdoor usages, a wealthy suburban dweller's per-capita usage could rise to 350 litres. And the change in climate, which is forecast to raise temperatures by 2-3 degrees Celsius over the next 75 years, is expected to bring deeper droughts, longer heat waves, water shortages, forest fires and inevitably, worst of all for the city dwellers, health problems. Each dry winter causes major depression'.

'I think we should change the subject. I'll have to go shortly for my flight'.

It was late that evening by the time Nurettin reached his home in Istanbul. After having dinner, Arzu was trying to switch off from work by reading, but thoughts related to work kept arriving and needed to be addressed, distracting her from her book. She waited up but was resigned to Nurettin arriving late and she started preparing for bed. Eventually after waiting too long, she retired to bed but could not sleep. Just for once she ignored her own best interests as she needed to be up at 6am the following morning, and decided that she wanted to be awake when Nurettin finally came home. The contents of a telephone call with her mother earlier that evening weighed heavily on her mind. She heard his key in the front door lock.

'Good day?' she asked immediately. She'd rehearsed her argument a hundred times, at least ten times that day, she just needed to move quickly through the pleasantries, an exchange of politeness undertaken each time they re-acquainted themselves, no matter how late in the day.

'Ok,....long, what about you?' he replied.

'We had the meeting with Ozel, it went OK, budget agreed for another year. I think I have done my bit with them and can afford to take a back seat.'

'How's that?' Nurettin was curious that all of a sudden Arzu didn't have the appetite to be the pioneering market expansionist.

'My mother called'.

'What is her news?'

'Not a lot, you know, my mother, asking me....*blaming* me'. Although there was a lot of padding surrounding the discussion the core topic was the perennial one, why was she still childless? It was not easy to speak to her parents on the telephone, let alone see them. Her achievements, apart from her marriage, did not seem to register with her parents. Instead she was destined to be burdened with guilt of childlessness. She loved being around children....for limited periods...other people's. But other people's children had begun to become a barrier between her and one or two of her closest friends, one-to-one conversations were suddenly cut short and never resumed or, in wider gatherings, roaming physical presences had to be reined in or attended to with more focus than even a prospective lover.

Moreover there was, to date, no pressure from Nurettin. At least no pressure that he had communicated to her verbally or demonstrably, but sometimes she thought she was meant to feel it through telepathy. Indeed on several occasions he had said it would be fine if it was just the two of them. This was a topic that, bizarrely, they had not discussed before they were married. Since then, her preferred position was to remain silent on the subject. Maybe she had misread the contract which stated that she had to offer Nurettin a child without discussion or she mistook him to be more gracious and informal than he really was. Suddenly there was likely to be an explosion out of which context he would make his feelings known. Or else there was no advance on a hollow separation for a marriage that had not brought her the sense of closeness or security she had hoped it would.

'If we're starting a family, I'd like to have the first one before I'm thirty'.

'Not now', Nurettin tried to convey the appearance of someone overcome by fatigue. Arzu, surprised at receiving a quick comment, could have been mistaken for thinking that Nurettin had said yes to the idea of having children sometime in the future.

After a long pause he said, 'You hadn't ever mentioned that you wanted a family'. There was something about the way he said it that Arzu interpreted he was saying no, he didn't want to have children or, at least, not with her. There was already a chasm between them. She considered several options; the possibility of bringing a child into the world against the wishes of an unenthusiastic father, then the unpalatable consequence that he might ask her to abort the foetus; the route of separation and divorce and finding someone else whom she liked and who did have paternal instincts. A life alone without a loving partner, or children, seemed momentarily unbearable. She could count on the fingers of one hand her friends who were in long-term relationships but who didn't have kids; one had decided her husband could never be a good father and another whose fear of giving birth was so intense that the couple decided to remain childless.

As Nurettin moved out of the bedroom into the living room, Arzu was happy to be alone with her thoughts as she tried to consider the positives of a lifetime with Nurettin, but without children, how she could maximise the opportunities provided by her work, unencumbered by attachments. There would be no shortages of places to go to, new people to meet and, at least for now, no shortage of social invitations.

She joined Nurettin in the living room to make sure he heard, 'if a mother is more than someone who has children then could it be that I'm more than someone who doesn't?', before returning to bed.

6

RUINED STEP

Over the expanse of his huge American mahogany desk that he sat behind, Mehmet pretended this was the first time he had read through the document and expressed surprise to Jeder when he turned over the page. 'But you have avoided putting anything against my most important question?' Mehmet had heard about Hussein Yıldırım's huge American mahogany desk and now he had reached the pinnacle of his career ambition, he was determined that he would have the biggest American mahogany desk made that could fit in his office.

From time to time he tried to conceal the smile of someone who knows he holds the better hand at cards, waiting for Jeder's reaction to the situation. Mehmet would slide sideways the middle finger of his right hand along the desktop in a straight line for a foot or so, as if to demonstrate the smoothness of the finish and then he would return along the same line with his right thumb, as if to protect the desk from any damage he may have caused with his middle finger from the first stroke. 'So you seem to have nearly all the answers. Did Hakan help you with this?'

Jeder gazed over at the prominent picture on the small circular reading light table by the side of Mehmet's huge desk. It showed Mehmet, his wife and their daughter at her graduation ceremony. In the photograph Mehmet exuded an air of impregnability and respectability that Jeder could never hope to emulate in his home country.

Mehmet wasn't excited by the status quo and thrived on crises. He quite liked to throw a terrier down the rabbit warren from time to time to keep his team on their toes. His staff, including Jeder, would run around for him twice as fast as they normally did. He could even persuade outside agencies to move quickly for him, such was his charm and directness and his ability to inculcate the notion that a common goodness would eventually prevail as the benefit of actions taken from his direction. He knew that the efficient and quickest way to enact change was against the background of a crisis. He savoured the moment when he would be able to describe to Hussein Yıldırım how his management had steered his ship away from a crisis, jettisoned some dead wood (there were always casualties in Mehmet's reconstructions) and sailed into calmer waters with freshly stocked cargo and a more motivated and alert crew. He just wanted to tell it, even though Hussein Yıldırım's indifference hardly disguised the fact that everyone knew who had presided over the circumstances that led to the crisis in the first place. Nevertheless Hussein Yıldırım couldn't fail to be impressed by the fact that Mehmet was able to implement real change, knew it would be painful and make him unpopular with some people forever, but drove it through regardless. At least Mehmet could tell it to Orhan *Bey*. There aren't many crises bigger than the aftermath of a major earthquake and look how well Mehmet had managed that. Nobody, not even his fiercest critics, could say that Mehmet had engineered that. He had reparations to his own company buildings completed in a matter of days and all employees back at work within a week, although most of them would retreat from the office to their homes whenever there were aftershocks. He also concluded early some unprofitable contracts without paying compensation and negotiated new loans underwritten by the safest banks; Nurettin's French bank had been involved in that. He also terminated the employment of three senior managers and promoted another to the board. Other companies took months of consultation and prevarication. But his biggest coup had been persuading Hussein Yıldırım to agree to a large company donation to provide materials for a new house building programme for families displaced as a result of the earthquake. He also volunteered several of his building services staff to support with the construction of these several hundred properties, activities that they assumed with relish. Although there were occasional periods after that when Mehmet's company didn't make a profit, his philanthropy was heavily publicised and he had cultivated many new contacts that recognised he was someone to whom you would give a chance in future.

Tamer had asked his staff to work until 9pm on the Wednesday evening after Jeder's call to corroborate the information they had previously supplied to Jeder, and some analysis information that Tamer thought he would never have to pass on to anybody. Tamer hadn't needed a call from Mehmet and deliberately surprised Jeder by supplying all the information he required. However Tamer did expect, at the very least, a visit by Jeder to the Ayvalık office to personally thank all those involved in the research and for him to buy them all lunch...when he had the time.

'I don't want to make up an answer, we must have the information?' Mehmet thought about the industrious women in the olive groves near Çanakkale, perched precariously on top of ladders, balancing their big collecting baskets while stretching to reach the branches, whilst other women on the ground combed the olives off the lower branches into a large net suspended under the trees. He liked their easy camaraderie as they joked and bantered with each other. Why couldn't it be like this with his office staff in Istanbul?

Mehmet hesitated, which was his way of telling Jeder to invent an answer that he would be held responsible for if it was subsequently found to be factually incorrect. Mehmet then appeared to sift randomly through the rest of Jeder's answers. He smiled as he saw on his desk the calling card of his favourite restaurant in Trabzon. He liked the ritual, on entering the restaurant, of being asked to remove any guns and leave them on the round table near the entrance before anybody could sit down for their meal; they picked them up again on their way out, handing the check-out person a tip as they also retrieved their coat from the stand next to the table. He pecked over a few more pages, like a mother blackbird organising her plump short-tailed hen chick before making her maiden flight. 'We have so many good restaurants in Istanbul and in the rest of the country', he muttered to himself.

'I am happy with the rest of the answers', which should have meant that was the end of the meeting. 'Wait a minute', Mehmet's attention had been drawn to the name of Ozel in the client list of affected accounts.

'*Şimdi*'. Mehmet looked at Jeder as if he had abused a member of his family. This was one of the bigger olive oil contracts that Mehmet's company had executed. Mehmet reckoned his company was facilitating about 15% of Ozel's annual exports of olive oil. The Ozel family was highly respected, its trading company's stock was quoted on the Turkish stock exchange and its publicity was proud to quote that it was the biggest producer of Turkish olive oil. Turkey was the fifth or sixth biggest producer of olive oil globally and there was a government drive to become second largest, after Spain. To do this, Italy and Greece would need to be overtaken and those countries were producing roughly double Turkey's output. As well as financial incentives the government provided a subsidy to support the olive tree growers in the south-west. Despite the fact that the subsidy was to help cover the cost of planting and cultivation in the first few years before the trees begin to bear fruit, the calculation of the subsidy for the growers supplying the Ozel family was based on export sales pricing information supplied by Mehmet's firm, figures provided under Jeder's supervision.

'Are you going to put me in an uncomfortable position?, Mehmet enquired. He could see Jeder grappling with the words to put the most favourable perspective on the situation. Jeder thought to himself, 'you don't know the half of it'.

'They obviously want to see the origin of our pricing. I didn't provide them with anything so far.

But we are obliged to supply them with it - everything we have by Friday night. I am sure they will want to review the traceability of the growers input prices to Ozel through to our export prices. Presumably they want our part and then they will go and see Ozel for the rest of it, to see if their information concurs.'

'Hakan worked on the pricing tables, didn't he?' Mehmet wanted to establish whether Hakan was complicit or whether Jeder had misrepresented or even forged Hakan's good work.

'I made some adjustments to what Hakan prepared', Jeder volunteered.

'*Yani*?'

'Meaning, I needed to offer us some protection'.

'How big?', Mehmet believed that tolerances could be easily explained by experts in the business to the governmental inspectors. But his facial expression (the nearest his rounded and generous face could twist into a frown) made it quite evident that he didn't approve of Jeder performing this practice, at least without consulting him first.

'Maximum 10%', Jeder thought that capping the error of judgement would calm Mehmet. In reality, for some of the heavy late summer months' deliveries made in the previous year the variance was nearer 20%, the discrepancy being required for the extractions to Nurettin's account. Jeder had become greedy and overconfident and had thought

113

that he could even manipulate the government aid contracts to line Nurettin's purse.

'Did you show Hakan what you had done?', Mehmet thought it was far too risky that Jeder had done this unilaterally, he just didn't know the Turkish market as well as Hakan.

'No, I didn't seek his opinion on all the adjustments', as scheming as Jeder was he felt he couldn't betray his loyal adjutant.

'Are you going to make me look foolish?', Mehmet had cooled a little, he leant back in his chair and his shoulders adopted a relaxed, resigned position. He felt that a mistake had been made but that it could be explained away; excessively volatile market conditions had been driven by the unexpected frosts in the spring, followed immediately by prolonged spells of torrential rain that had stunted the size of the olives at last year's harvest.

'I will gather all the documents and files and share them with you before I hand them over to the Unit', Jeder offered Mehmet the chance to check everything before it left the building.

'Everything must be on paper, no hard drives', Mehmet said in a quiet, measured fashion to ensure there could be no misunderstanding. 'Azize!' he shouted, unsure if she was at her desk in the adjoining room or not. He looked down at the vast expanse of his desk top and then spoke so quietly that only Jeder could hear him 'When the hearing takes place-probably next week, you and I will both attend; you'd better sharpen your understanding of Turkish'.

'Azize!!' he shouted louder and with more urgency. If she was not at her desk then she should have been, and if she was down the corridor she would be sure to come running. Jeder could almost hear Azize wincing and sighing, as she returned to her office in time to hear the second demand, not appreciating being shouted at, and then she came through into Mehmet's office.

'Azize', now in a much softer and more civil tone, 'please ask Taner to come to my office'.

'You have Orhan *Bey* in five minutes, here is your signature book and I have more applications for the security guard post', it wouldn't be appropriate to keep Orhan *Bey* waiting while Mehmet interrogated Taner and finished with Jeder.

'*Tamam*', Mehmet knew Azize would process the instruction and he was confident Taner would make it upstairs to Mehmet's office within a minute and then he would still have time to finish with Jeder in a couple of minutes. Azize promptly summoned Taner.

Mehmet and Jeder sat in silence for a few moments. Jeder looking anywhere but at Mehmet. 'Taner!', Mehmet shouted as he heard Taner approaching his door but before he could see him.

'Evet, efendim'.

Mehmet raised his head from the documents on his desk and gave Taner an old-fashioned look when he saw he was wearing bright yellow corduroy trousers. 'Taner, please bring me the Ozel contract file, with the schedule attachments for each of the past three years, starting with 1999'. Mehmet didn't have to say by when he needed this, he knew that Taner would bring the documents immediately and they would be deposited with Azize while Mehmet was having his meeting with Orhan *Bey*. It was Mehmet's style to ask other people for corroborating evidence. Jeder knew how simple a task this was for Mehmet as he commanded unwavering respect from his subordinates.

'Yes, you can do that' Mehmet continued where he had left off with Jeder but now speaking quite clearly so Azize in the next room would be sure to hear, 'but I am going to receive their official requirements latest by tomorrow. You can begin to prepare all your detailed documents. It doesn't seem as though we will have any case to answer but for sure we will have to attend this hearing. This will not be a criminal trial, more like a declaration. You and I will *both* have to attend', Mehmet's emphasis on the word *both* made it clear to Jeder that this incident had been provoked by Jeder himself and was now going to deflect his boss away from more important matters. Mehmet harboured a far-fetched thought that Jeder, as a foreign national, might somehow be implicated in the trial and that he could be extradited to the UK, so some good might come out of this after all. Jeder could be deported, Mehmet contemplated; Jeder wouldn't be able to claim he had a right to a family life in Turkey; he wasn't married to a Turkish woman, at least not yet. The activities outside the office were something Mehmet couldn't quite control.

Then in swept Azize again into Mehmet's office.

'Orhan *Bey* is waiting to see you'.

'Ah', Mehmet stood up and made to move over to the big round table, at which a more cordial discussion could take place. Jeder's time was up and as he moved towards the door Mehmet threw him 'It's a five week month, you are way behind target'. Jeder acknowledged him without saying how the situation would be redressed. 'But I think you should take a few days away from Istanbul. Why don't you go to Trabzon to review your rice project?'

The activity in Mehmet's room then resembled the end of an act in a play as Azize gathered, and then took out with her, props to change the scenery for Orhan *Bey's* arrival; Mehmet's document signature book, the tea glasses and coffee cups were swept away, trade magazines shuffled and tidied, even the lights were lowered, the curtains came down and the audience retired to the bars for some light refreshment.

Orhan *Bey* had been instructed by Hussein Yıldırım to review and clear for publication Mehmet's internal communication. That took about five minutes and for the rest of the meeting they were able to exchange pleasantries about various members of their respective families.

After Orhan *Bey* had left and before lunch Mehmet had issued the statement, 'Some of you may have heard that we are under investigation by government authorities. There are discussions currently proceeding with management and at this point we do not expect other members of staff to be involved. There is no cause for alarm. If anyone has any questions please address them to me'. As a coda to the bulletin, Mehmet added, 'We are confident that these discussions will result in a satisfactory outcome for the company'. Mehmet asked Azize to share with him what she had heard but she said that she hadn't heard anything; Mehmet couldn't fathom whether she was telling the truth, although why she should cover for Jeder was beyond him.

The last thing Mehmet wanted was to implicate the company in the cost and uncertainty of a Turkish court and then, possibly, later a US jury trial (should the US government have been, in some way, cheated by the impact of these related transactions). Mehmet later discussed the matter directly with Hussein Yıldırım rather than using Orhan *Bey* as a go-between. Hussein Yıldırım said he would ask around but privately he didn't think it was any concern of his, it was a local matter that Mehmet should deal with.

If Jeder was asked, he would propagate the thought that there had been a misconception and that nothing untoward had taken place; this was in keeping with the cold flat words of the company statement. He felt he could say that without any necessity to elaborate further. Just in the same way Jeder didn't understand the recent spate of stoppages due to union action driven by the reaction to the Gunay deal.

At lunchtime, instead of heading for the canteen, Jeder left the office and went out in search of a newspaper to try to find out other perspectives on the Gunay affair. Instead the banner headlines were all about the armed forces resisting the influence of Islam in education. It seemed nobody in Turkey wanted the army back in charge. Deputies had voted overwhelmingly in favour of the legislation which would ease restrictions on students of religious vocational schools entering university. This had been causing an outcry in the universities. Furthermore, the military was concerned. The cause of the controversy was a clause in the bill that would grant equal university access to religiously educated high school students. At that time they were banned from going to secular universities and from pursuing careers as public officials. It was widely expected to be vetoed for fear of creeping Islamisation. The general staff of the armed forces claimed that the bill would undermine the secular republic.

Of the people Jeder knew in Turkey he felt compelled to tell Nurettin; the arrangement with Nurettin forced him out of bed each morning and fuelled him with optimism before he went to sleep each night. He hadn't seen Nurettin for a week and a half.

That evening after he had reached home he dialled Nurettin's number. He never called Nurettin from the office, it was already difficult sharing an office with Hakan and Hakan's assistant to be able to make any discreet telephone calls. Jeder would sometimes miss lunch to do this, which left him listless and inefficient in the afternoon. He was acutely aware of how office performance plummeted in the month of Ramadan, especially when it fell in the summer; measured against that, his own food and drink lunchtime hiatus every once in a while was microscopic.

As the phone started to ring Jeder only had one thought in his head. that Nurettin would not be happy if he thought that Jeder had been defrauding the Turkish government. The phone rang about seven times then Jeder suddenly recalled that Nurettin had said he was going to be in Spain that week; he was glad to slam down the handset before someone might pick up.

He cast around for his pocket diary. There were no pictures of his family in the house. He had already been working in Turkey for three years on secondment from his US employers. He had pictures of his first wife and their two sons when they were babies but no pictures of the two boys on their own. It had never been appropriate to frame the group pictures of his wife and the boys whilst he was living with Gail and he hadn't managed to do it since he had moved to Turkey. His house was already a soulless concrete prison, with its white interior walls, but Jeder had augmented the lack of humanity with his artless efforts on the walls, side tables, cabinets and dressers. 'Nurettin back from Spain' was one of the diary entries for the coming Friday. So the earliest he was able to meet with Nurettin was the following Saturday. Nurettin had been away in Spain on holiday during the week. Jeder was unsure how he was going to survive the week, what was going to happen if the Special Investigation Unit escalated their enquiries. He started thinking what he was going to do if he had to commit to statements of fact without having had a chance to clear them with Nurettin beforehand.

He had never been completely straightforward with Nurettin about exactly how he managed to channel around US$ 10,000 a month into the Içecek account. Similarly, he had been economical with the truth when he explained to Mehmet that margins on the Aegean portfolio were re-based at a lower level than the five year average, citing fluctuating origin prices driven by major variations in the annual Turkish output; Jeder could only think that Mehmet's concerns were assuaged by the fact that over that five year period his company had increased its share of the olive oil export market. Whilst Mehmet might have been concerned that Jeder was letting increased margin opportunities escape by not expertly anticipating trends and that might result in a tolerable rebuke, should Nurettin discover that Jeder had been defrauding the government he may as well have been bound in a straitjacket, standing on a trap door above a pit full of vipers with Nurettin's hand on the trap-fall lever.

The following morning Jeder rose early and prepared his bag for a three day trip to the North-East coast. He called the taxi company to be at his house at 6.30 am to take him to the airport.

There was still no sign of Hakan, neither at check-in nor boarding. Maybe he'd entered the plane early and was right at the back. Almost everyone on the plane looked like they had business in Trabzon, there were no tourists.

Jeder sat next to someone who possessed an almost identical annoying habit as Nurettin. Out of his computer bag he decanted papers, notes, invoices, air ticket stubs, receipts, a playing card and some noteletes. The irritating part was with each noteletes he chuckled before ripping it up; like he was loving the fact that he was having a good time but you were definitely excluded. Then he stuffed the resultant debris into the seat pocket in front of him. As the seat pocket was a net with large holes, a lot of the shredded paper ended up under his feet on the cabin floor. While it seemed this man performed this ritual just as demonstrably and as nosily as Nurettin, you could be sure that Nurettin would capture the torn pieces of paper neatly and secure them all in a small side pocket of his laptop bag.

The former Turkish Air Force pilot seemed to be doing a wonderful job negotiating the 737 into Trabzon airport amid a heavy storm. It was always raining whenever Jeder's plane approached Trabzon. The mountains, dark and brooding, loomed large as they impinged on to the sea.

Invariably when 10,300 metres up, with the temperature at -43 degrees Celsius outside, travelling at 900 kilometres per hour but into a 150 kilometres per hour headwind, Jeder was unable to prevent idle speculation about a problem. Each jerk, jump and bounce through the clouds, or the sweeping run up through warm air to pockets of very cold air, could be the catalyst that would drop an engine or lose part of the tail fin or at least an engine cowling. He was steadily becoming more paranoid about air travel. He hadn't seen it scientifically proved, but from his own recent flight experiences he was unable to recall a flight without some episode of violent turbulence, and this certainly hadn't been the case when he started travelling ten years previously. Five years earlier in his old job, he had started badgering an Estonian colleague to give him updates each time before he flew.

Tõnis knew all about the European airline fleets, the type of the aircraft they used, the experience and background of the pilots, the ages of the aircraft and their safety records, particularly those of the ex-Soviet countries. He also knew approximately the state of their finances, roughly how much it cost to lease new aircraft and what proportion of their costs they purported to spend on aircraft maintenance. Most of the ex-Soviet countries, of course, now had brand new fleets and excellent pilots. Tõnis also knew the airports with the difficult landings and take-offs, the ones that were built too near mountains and the ones where it was at times foggy, so flights were delayed. He also knew the ones which used the same inefficient, but people-saving, bagging handling systems and could give estimates about the minimum time you would have to wait for your checked-in baggage. Jeder recalled the information that Tõnis routinely relayed, one cabin crew for 1 to 50 passengers, two for 51 to 100 passengers, 3 for etc.

In the absence of news from Tõnis, Jeder read with morbid fascination every published account of aviation investigations into civil incidents. Although he felt more confident with Turkish Airlines than almost every other carrier, Jeder could not help running a scenario when this 737 would veer suddenly to the left and unavoidably slam into the Trabzon hillside, killing everybody on board. Would the subsequent protracted international investigation reveal that the plane had not been properly maintained and was unfit to fly? Or would the statement say that the cause of the crash has yet to be identified, but there was conjecture that the crash was caused by unusually bad weather conditions? The manufacturer and aviation experts would state that the safety record of that particular plane was exemplary and it had been serviced and maintained appropriately in line with manufacturing guidelines and aviation industry best practice. In the background was the possible pilot error, caused by fatigue, after flying for a period exceeding what is acceptable under international aviation law. Or would the cause of the crash be overshadowed by the accusations of negligence and misconduct aimed at the Turkish government? Especially when forensic reports revealed that Turkish military personnel had misidentified 15 of the victims' bodies before they were repatriated to various European countries. One consistent thread with other crashes was that no member of the public could ever recall the official verdict of the enquiry.

Would there be anyone there to mourn or to grieve or to pity when Jeder's casket made its way back to Heathrow? Would there be anyone there detailed by the Foreign Office to review and check the forensic records? What about someone there who would be affected by the macabre mix-up of bodies which saw Jeder's remains from seat 17C replaced by those of a Dane in seat 5F but that both men´s checked-in baggage were recorded in Jeder's name? Would anybody check the autopsy records in the morgue in Trabzon, even years later?

The sudden sight of land through the porthole window snapped Jeder back from his idle reverie. On several occasions the plane seemed to be just about to land in the sea and then suddenly there was a runway below and the plane dropped down on to it with the noise of a big slamming metallic door; the impact banging the crockery, cutlery, bottles and glasses in the metal trolleys stowed away towards the front of the plane.

As the plane turned and taxied to the stand, Jeder speculated on the next part of the journey, moving eastwards from Trabzon to the Georgian border and the expectation that he would see tea bushes and hazelnut forests all over the hillsides; but that he still wouldn't be able to make time to see the Sümela monastery, suspended on the side of a rock spur in the Pontic mountains. This was about 50 kilometres from Trabzon, and not on their route. Nor any time to reach Vazelon and Peristera before those remains disintegrated completely in the Pontic foothills.

When Jeder came through the airport concourse, Hakan was there to meet him, and as if by way of excuse of all that had gone before, and to absolve himself from his absence from the office and lack of communication, he was the first to speak.

'The itinerary has changed'. Hakan passed Jeder a single page with the revised list of sites they were going to visit. Hakan was of medium height, dark hair but no moustache, with a pleasant but not striking face. Like Jeder, he was also in his late thirties but looked younger because of his slight build and his habit of dressing in teenagers' clothes. When the two of them approached a stranger together, Jeder would always be addressed first even though he looked like a foreigner. This pleased Jeder a lot even if the conversation would be re-directed to Hakan almost immediately.

'Oh yes? Have you caught up yet with what happened in the office over the past couple of weeks?' Jeder barely contained his stored impatience with Hakan.

'I thought that had all blown over', Hakan said casually, as the two men made their way out of the airport towards a waiting car, Jeder dragging a 20 kilo bag behind him. Hakan had long ceased feeling responsible for Jeder as a stranger in a strange land. He only briefly speculated on how the bag could weigh so much and its contents not be identified by the airport x-ray machines and confiscated.

'N-o', Jeder elongated the tiny word and made it sound tired and last as long as possible, 'this could explode...'.

When they reached the Honda there was already a driver in the front passenger seat and two hefty men in the back seat. Hakan took extra care not to hurt his back as he wedged Jeder's case into the trunk alongside the gas tank and ushered him into the front passenger seat. The driver moved over into the driving seat to accommodate Jeder. Hakan closed the trunk and sat behind the driver so he could more easily converse with Jeder. The three men were wedged together in the back seat, so even if they didn't want to be touching the man next to them it wasn't possible.

'They're going to have our guts for garters', Hakan didn't need to know precisely what Jeder meant but he could tell by his awkwardness that there was going to be a bill to be paid somehow. After all, the rumour mill in the office was unerring in its judgement about who was the cause of the issue. Jeder was keen to put some hot coals under someone else's feet.

'It's quite possible...', Jeder continued but he was cut short as the driver interrupted them asking Hakan for clarification on the directions. This gave Hakan the excuse to say that he hadn't heard what Jeder had said, or more precisely, to explain what he meant by 'could explode' or 'garters'. But before he was able to say anything Jeder resumed, '...that these government officials already know too much'.

Hakan told him he should take them seriously, it wasn't clear how they would react or whether they would eventually take action against him. No mud was sticking and the SIU problem continued to be uniquely Jeder's domain.

'Things like this happen in Turkey because we do not have up-to-date rules for corporate governance ', Hakan moved into a high-handed, slightly sneering mode, 'think about the Balım case from a few years back. There is nothing to regulate where people like the Balım brothers can and cannot invest their money and where they can utilise their resources'.

'Yes, but this is quite different', Jeder countered, 'in this case it is not clear whose money it is we are talking about. Is it the state's, is it ours, or should it belong to the olive oil producers?' as the car took a sudden left turn and the men's combined weight shifted with it, Jeder could see Hakan's face banging into the side window and his furrowed brow could either have represented the reaction to a bruised nose or the realisation that he was going to have to listen to Jeder for the next twenty minutes. 'The ambiguity in the scheme', Jeder continued, comfortably in the front seat, 'means that no one is quite sure. Lawyers might become involved. We are taking advantage, at least for the moment, that no one quite knows the way it works. Mehmet's quite clear about that'.

'In the Balım affair', Jeder addressed Hakan's diversion, 'the banking watchdog was able to seize one of the two banks controlled by their group and rake over all the dealings that had gone on to find the perpetrators. That is no precedent for this case'.

As the jalopy made off up into the hills Hakan intended to close the conversation, convinced that the Turkish way of doing things was correct and that justice would prevail, whatever the ramifications might be for Jeder, 'None of us applauded the way that the Balım brothers had been carrying on. It just became another deterrent for foreign investors putting more money in our country'.

Then half way up the hill, or so Jeder thought, the driver abruptly pulled over to the side and stopped the car. The two large men, acknowledging the driver, stepped out of the car and made their way over to a small complex of modern houses. Hakan found himself alone in the back of the Honda.

The new itinerary meant they had to fit in a visit to the tea institute in Rize. They were soon driving on undulating, deserted roads away from urbanisations. A further twenty minutes later they were passing through areas of orchards and forests of chestnut and alder which covered the remote valleys in a thick mantle of green. Hakan asked the driver to stop several times so they could inspect some impressive buildings, occasionally a magnificent mansion or farmhouse constructed of timber and stone. Jeder produced his tourist camera from the huge case in the trunk.

Even though Jeder had understood from the original itinerary that Azize had passed him, that the only good hotels were in and around Rize, they drove straight through that town and along the coast road to Fındıklı. The endless deep-green tea plantations covered the slopes of the hills outside Rize. In the small coastal towns they drove through, at the side of the road there were women, young and old, who worked the plantations, supporting conical baskets on their backs, waiting for their leaves to be collected.

Then the car turned off the coastal road inland to the Çağlayan valley. It was an area quite deserted of people. City life had lured away the descendants of the men and women who built these properties. Inheritance laws divided and then divided again the ownership, so it was diluted to such an extent that no individual could take on the responsibility of repairing and maintaining them. Tea had been first planted in this area in the 1930s and it was easy to imagine how local residents had prospered for a while. Some of the tea plantations surrounding some of the bigger houses continued to be cultivated, while many of these beautiful houses lay abandoned. Inside the houses, wood had been used not only for the doors but also for the internal walls and ceilings. The doors themselves were carved with stylised patterns of exotic plants and fruit.

In the back seat Hakan began to rehearse aloud his conversation with the hotel manager, who he made sound like a Sikh, perhaps from a film Hakan had seen. 'We would like two big rooms but they need to be airy, quiet and above all clean with comfortable beds'.

'Our best rooms are on the second floor, sir. I can assure you all our rooms are clean, have comfortable beds and are well insulated against noise from adjacent rooms. At the moment I have 205 and 206 available. 205 has more interesting antique furniture and *objets d`art* but room 206 benefits from more natural light'.

'Well let me see the rooms then'.

As the battered Honda turned off the made-up road and slithered up a dirt track, Jeder and Hakan both hoped the driver knew the lane well as he gave the car more momentum than felt comfortable or safe on a blind sharp corner. They came to a dramatic halt and the Çağlayan mansion sprung into view, situated in front of a dramatic rising hill planted with tea. Jeder said, 'I don't think there is a room 205 or 206 here'.

The feature of the garden of the house was the literally translated 'ruined step'. This was a spot atop a long stone wall of about a metre and a half in height. It was said that on this point of the wall the merchant who constructed the house used to stand and contemplate his estate. The step was 'ruined' because the merchant eventually bankrupted himself through over ambition or ill fortune. You had to assume the merchant was both young and agile because it would be difficult enough to vault up on to the top of the wall, but stabilising and then balancing yourself on top of it would be a further challenge. There was nothing to hang on to once you were standing on the wall. Of course as it was bad luck to repeat the stance of the merchant, most visitors contented themselves with placing their right hand rather than their right boot on top of the wall at the appropriate mark, this action was not meant to bring bad luck. So that while the 'step' where the merchant might have placed his right boot was well defined, it was not at all clear where he might have placed his left boot to achieve the necessary balance to stand on top of his wall for any length of time. Surely not long enough anyway to bring him that much bad luck. You could only imagine he had over reached himself on one of his trips to Russia bringing back more spoils than he had paid for and suffering the consequences. Retribution would have been felt on that house or inside it.

Jeder invariably slept badly on a first night in new surroundings. That night was no exception. He was not great at sharing a room either, as he was an excessively loud snorer, if he couldn't prop up his head and neck with sufficient pillows. Hakan also snored and appeared to enjoy a more contented sleep as far as Jeder could tell.

As they entered the room Jeder glanced over at Hakan and said, 'They are going to find us'.

There was no response from Hakan. Sometimes Jeder babbled away in English with his Mancunian accent knowing that Hakan was only catching one word in four. It was impossible to frighten Hakan with words.

'They're going to catch us in our sleep. They're going to cut our throats'. Hakan surmised that Jeder was referring to the Ozel business.

There was no lock on the door and the windows could be opened from the outside. They were open to the elements.

'But we're on the second floor', insisted Hakan, looking out of the window and content that the drop to the ground was far enough.

'People can easily climb up the stairs and open our door.'

Hakan looked at Jeder communicating with disbelieving eyes that people just wouldn't do that here.

'You can have the bed nearest the door', Jeder gestured to the smaller of the two beds, after all Hakan was smaller than him, 'in case you need to use the bathroom in the middle of the night.' This is what Jeder must have meant by 'taking it for the team'. Even though the 'team' was never any bigger than Hakan and himself.

Jeder always slept with a hammer under his bed. Not that he ever had to use it. Sometimes he thought about Arzu's brothers, her cousins and her uncles, all coming after him, but Arzu's husband was always in the background detached from, but perhaps the instigator of, the action. He'd brought the hammer with him to Trabzon. Comparing notes, Nurettin had told Jeder that he always slept with a fire extinguisher living in permanent fear of an arson attack.

As Jeder carefully paced the wooden floor of the room in the night in his sock-less shoes trying to make himself tired enough to fall asleep, Hakan didn't stir. There were no carpets, kilims or rugs and Jeder didn't trust the floor to be devoid of splinters. As it was, the night passed without incident, but as Jeder awoke he sensed he had been in court again

135

and was desperately trying to remember the whole content of his most recent dream.

Slumbering in the few minutes before his alarm was due to go off, Jeder had been toying with the concept of revealing to Hakan exactly what he had been doing with the olive oil price declarations. Would it have been better to have taken Hakan into his confidence, could he trust him not to tell anyone? Jeder would have to pay him off. He knew Hakan a little but couldn't judge whether his honour would preclude him from accepting any bribe. Alternatively, Jeder could blindly proceed, deceiving Hakan, Mehmet, Nurettin, eventually the SIU and anyone else he came across. Perhaps Hakan already knew, had already told Mehmet but it suited Mehmet for the moment to stay quiet. After all, businesses under-reported crime discovered within their own organisations, either because they don't know what's happening or they are afraid to admit it, lest it lay bare their own management and supervisory failings. He couldn't be sure which way Mehmet would flip when he found out, but he knew whatever action taken would be decisive....probably using the discovery as an excuse to ask for Jeder to quietly withdraw from the business and for him and his associates to refund all monies they had misappropriated.

Before he had refreshed and showered and started to dress, Jeder determined that he couldn't shoulder his burden alone, he was going to involve Hakan.

However by the time he made it to breakfast, Jeder had decided to change his story which conformed more with the tale that he was telling Nurettin, that he was defrauding the Turkish government for the benefit of Mehmet initially; Jeder said that he had begun by extracting funds from the Turkish government subsidy scheme but had later channelled them through Mehmet's company and on to a third party.

'The scheme started off as a subsidy for Mehmet', he'd broken the seal of his agreement with Nurettin, no turning back now, 'to help the financial position. These type of companies needed support from the state. I was doing it differently. After a while, I felt I was channelling too much money that Mehmet would notice and be embarrassed'.

'Embarrassed? More like volcanic'. Hakan moved into his comfort zone of having known Mehmet for a lot longer than Jeder had.

'So I began to divert funds out of Mehmet's company into a third party company'.

'To which you have access?'

'Not exactly'

'You do or you don't?'

'Yes....but not yet'. The blood drained from Hakan's face. He felt incompetent; having worked so closely with Jeder but never having identified what was happening. Now he was belittled and betrayed.

'How could you do this?' he stood up at the table, making as if to leave the breakfast room. He knew he didn't threaten Jeder physically but maybe he could disturb his conscience.

Jeder clenched the seat with his thighs and the edge of the table with his hands in a gesture to make Hakan sit down again, the revelation had to continue, there was more to come.

'I'm deciding how I am going to pay the money back', Jeder now really felt like he was making up the story as he went.

'Why did you take it out in the first place, how did you take it out?' Hakan, still standing and requiring a full apology to him, gave the impression he could leave right then and there, go back to Istanbul and spill the beans to Mehmet, such as he had been slighted.

Realising it would be painful for Hakan to be revealed as an unwitting accomplice in the deed of extracting the funds from Mehmet's company, Jeder tried to proceed with his own dilemma and the fact that he was about to lean on Hakan for a favour.

'I need to work out how to bring the funds back into the company', this comment still didn't make Hakan take his seat.

'You no longer *have* the money', Hakan bent down and almost put his face in Jeder's before moving away and making for the stairs to the room.

Jeder carried on eating his breakfast of bread and fruit. He could see a long day ahead of him and would eat everything in front of him to build up his strength. He felt confident Hakan wasn't going to dash out of the house, he was too professional to abandon the day they had planned, and Jeder wasn't going to give himself indigestion chasing Hakan upstairs to the room.

When Jeder returned to their room Hakan had gone but by the time Jeder had packed up and was outside the front of the house again, Hakan was there talking to a driver.

In the same Honda, a different driver was waiting for them, as if the previous one believed he was transporting damaged goods and couldn't carry on. Some drivers might feel privileged carrying a suitcase full of bank notes in the trunk; but not this one. 'Am I taking you all the way to Zonguldak?' Hakan hesitated to climb into the car saying to himself 'I think we have the wrong car', and then seeing there were no other vehicles around, he gave the driver a doubtful look 'Other direction. I'll tell you where to go'.

As they set out, at first Hakan would not engage Jeder in conversation, he just looked out of the car window into the distance. Hakan hadn't yet defined what would be his new role, blackmailer, friend, fixer, ex-colleague, prison visitor.

Visiting the tea institute reminded Jeder of his purpose here in Turkey. While masquerading behind olive oil trading, his main interest was in research into rice yields. Having funding from the Turkish government via the Mediterranean Region Cooperative Research Network on Rice, enabled Hakan and Jeder to research the effect of global warming on rice crop yields. Even though Turkey only produced 70,000 metric tonnes, certain bright thinking individuals in the food institute in Ankara were prepared to spend money to have Turkish research up in lights on the subject of feeding the nation and maybe some of its neighbours. It had been tough gaining funding from Ankara. Day after day, week after week of day trips to Ankara, being prepared to wait long intervals in ante rooms before showing research credentials and petitioning civil servants.

Hakan directed the driver to the first test site. They were greeted by a small delegation of farmers and shepherded into an agricultural building containing a large table. Hakan and Jeder sat on one side, four farmers on the other. Hakan soon took over the talking from Jeder but the Mancunian fed him statements to translate into Turkish.

'Before we go out, from the reports we've received the crop varieties you are using are just too expensive. You're spending too much on pesticides and chemical fertilisers'. Jeder waited for Hakan to translate. Hakan spoke good English as he had lived and worked in North London from 1990-1993. Mehmet thought he would be a good fit for Jeder even if the cockney he had learned didn't prepare him for the Oldham accent from the North West of England. Before the farmers had a chance to respond, Jeder fuelled Hakan, 'You're missing the whole point of SRI. You're meant to use less seeds, less water and fewer chemicals to produce a better yield. This is why we are using this System of Root Intensification'.

Once Hakan had translated that, the farmers talked amongst themselves and their spokesman fired back at Hakan, who grudgingly said to Jeder, 'They say the land around Trabzon is not the best area for these tests'. He further volunteered, 'this is what Mehmet always said'. Tea was brought in as refreshment. 'The area in which rice can be sown cannot be increased because all available water here is fully committed. We need to be growing on heavy soils to minimize filtration'. Jeder was beginning to doubt whether Hakan was still with the project. Hakan still held in his back pocket the ability to make one phone call to Mehmet.

'I can't buy that excuse about the quality of the soil. This area near Trabzon that we've chosen has

141

some of the best growing conditions in the country', Jeder replied.

Over the previous two decades the average temperature had increased, particularly at night, and the rice yield had reduced as a result. For every one degree Celsius night- time increase, the yield of grain went down by 10 per cent. Mehmet had no interest in this research and just saw it as a drain on the bottom line. He couldn't possibly see how Turkey could become an important rice producer. A sizeable proportion of rice crops was established with aerial sowing, the schemes would be heavily capital intensive and unlikely to attract further immediate funding for the equipment to help increase the crop size; it was difficult to anticipate from where the momentum would come for the project.

Jeder had heard about and researched the SRI techniques developed in Asia, just recently since 1995, and was convinced this could be introduced to Turkey. The success of the project in the test area would not be so dependent on the quality of the soil, but relied more on the technique used to grow the rice. This was mainly about transplanting week-old seedlings into dry soil, keeping the area around the plants weeded and well spaced for aeration; rather than planting three week-old seedlings in clumps of three or four in waterlogged fields as was the traditional method.

'Could you tell them we've chosen them because we expect their better husbandry will give better yields'. Before Hakan translated this, he replied to Jeder, 'these growers are conservative and prefer to follow traditional rice growing techniques'.

'Tell them this is about better management practices rather than a revolution in growing techniques. It's very low cost, it is all based on training a few hundred people to teach SRI methods.'

Hakan's reply from the farmers came back, 'it's labour intensive back-breaking work to transplant the young rice shoots from the nursery beds to the paddy fields. Secondly it is problematical keeping the paddy fields properly irrigated'. The second reason was not insurmountable, Jeder surmised, the first was more about a desire to see the trials succeed.

'Talk to them about what our Dutch friend told us yesterday when we called him'.

'Growers have tried the SRI methods but not seen through with the trials', Hakan started to explain. 'They think that the SRI techniques are good for small families and village communities who use their own labour, but as soon as you try to expand the project onto a more industrial scale then they say labour becomes too expensive. The problem is nobody has invented the technology to transplant the single seedlings yet. The good news is that governments in India and Indonesia are starting to promote SRI and are putting money behind the education and training of farmers in these techniques, so there is some light at the end of the tunnel.'

The farmers grumbled so Jeder said to Hakan, 'we may find a bit more funding from abroad'. He knew this was unlikely as there was a growing resistance against scientists wanting to change the soil nutrients to improve yields. 'The Ankara grants have run out', Jeder shielded his mouth from the view of the farmers as if he was a tennis doubles player giving instructions to a partner, 'we can continue these trials for a little longer until there is risk of a frost. Tell them the trials continue'. Hakan relayed the information which appeared to be grudgingly accepted. The farmers had decided the meeting had ended and began to file out. Jeder and Hakan climbed back into the Honda.

The reception and discussion were the same at the two other test sites they visited. They made their way back to Trabzon airport for the return trip.

So, if Jeder had followed Mehmet's guidance he should have still been at his desk in Üsküsdar sorting through and removing potentially recriminating documents rather than being at rice farms in Trabzon. Jeder's rice project would be the first to be jettisoned, Jeder's travel expenses alone would save two people's salaries. What relevance

144

now the fixing of the price of olive oil? If it was in America there might have been a possibility for an out of court settlement but here, perhaps not.

Jeder was hoping his opportunity in Almaty would materialise before the SIU investigation revealed anything. The SIU file on him was only going to expand rather than contract, the Unit was not going to stay still after their initial findings. As it was, at least two of members of the board of Mehmet's company were already searching for jobs elsewhere. Mehmet, having faith in his own impregnability, would happily deal with that, as a separate crisis, should it ever surface.

Back in his Nişantaşı apartment Nurettin only fleetingly pondered that Jeder's deportation order might have been served at any moment. He was more worried that Jeder might not always have been a reliable partner; what was to stop Jeder leaving for Almaty right away, then his misdemeanours in Mehmet's company would come to light and the government would not only claw back all the transfers Jeder had engineered but also consign Nurettin to jail. Other, bigger, legitimate sources of income needed to be found. Nurettin just needed to dislocate Içecek Holdings so that there could be no trace to him. He now needed to pay more attention to Javier.

7

EXPECTED ARRIVAL

Aruş had been hammering on his door for weeks. 'Better do the bad part of the day first', Nurettin muttered to himself. He visited the Citibank ATM in Istinye for the third time that week, very early in the morning, to empty his US dollar account.

Long gone were the balmy August days. As recently as September he'd been swimming further up at the top of the Bosphorous, where a pod of dolphins had been cavorting nearby. Now, in late October, a cold mist shrouded the harbour in the early morning, and later in the day the dirty rain from the Black Sea would soak the whole city. He thought Aruş would be more impressed with hard currency than Lira; there must be more from where that had come; perhaps that would be enough to make him change his mind, once he had seen a duffle bag full of greenbacks.

He handed over the money to Aruş at 830am that Thursday outside the entrance to the Robert College in Arnavutkoy. His former friend said smugly, 'You see, you talked about the billions of dollars spent by the Turkish government on building dams. Supposedly to increase water reserves and increase hydroelectric capacity. Well, look what's happening now; these same projects are facing the prospect of delays; western companies are withdrawing their tenders, because of the adverse publicity on human rights. Money is not coming to Turkey'.

'I've seen it', Nurettin wiped his lips with the back of his hand as if *he'd* been the one spitting blood. 'Look, here is some of it', Aruş resisted Nurettin's attempt to snatch back the bag and open it. Nurettin stood back with his arms down by his side, 'Aren't you going to check it?'

'I trust you. I've always trusted you.' Aruş kept the bag tightly shut not wanting to lose anything. 'I just don't believe in your project'.

As Aruş turned to leave and walk down the street to catch a *dolmuş*, Nurettin looked to see if the small ruck sack on his back could be concealing a gun. Aruş' easy walk made it clear he was not encumbered by the task of killing anybody. Nurettin flagged down the first yellow cab to take him to Maslak.

It was a real coup securing a meeting at the Ministry of Forest and Water Management. The department was headquartered in Ankara but Nurettin had waited in vain for instructions to buy his air ticket. He was only permitted to meet a low ranking department official at a room in the Istanbul Technical University in Maslak. He didn't often go to Maslak but when he did he thought it was the Istanbul elders' attempt to create their version of Paris' *La Defense*. With its skyscrapers, huge modern courtyards and open spaces the project had started with plenty of ambition. Now Maslak was half-finished and under-built and was never even going to rival the more sophisticated banking complex in Levent. Although one thing he did know was that these skyscrapers would pass the earthquake tests.

He'd acquired this link through a work colleague whose father was employed by the state in Istanbul. As usual he had prepared immaculately; the commercial realisation of his masters' thesis on water gathering, distribution and consumption was always likely to gain him an audience. He just had to be sure he was talking to the right people.

In the courtyard outside the university building Nurettin felt proud to be living in a modern democracy, as clean-shaven men in ties and women in skirts busily went in and out; not a head scarf in sight. From where he was standing he couldn't even see a minaret. He felt confident springing up the steps, towards the revolving doors and through the security scanners.

He didn't have to wait long to be summoned to the office of a scientific consultant from the irrigation department who, by his diffidence, was keen to demonstrate to Nurettin that he was just one person in a long line and would need to be dealt with quickly. The official was male, in his mid-thirties, without a moustache and well-spoken. His white laboratory coat branded him a technician, but he had the air of a politician.

As always, unless he was speaking to Sibel Doğan, Nurettin felt he was at least the equal of a new acquaintance and wanted to be on the front foot with a bucket full of small talk.

'Which university did you attend?'

'It was here, I graduated with a degree in civil engineering'. For a moment, Nurettin saw him as a kindred spirit.

'Have you been here ever since?'

'No, I went abroad, to Delft in the Netherlands, to do research and post graduate studies'. Already the technician felt a little insulted that Nurettin might think his experience limited and he sat down to indicate that was the end of the preliminaries. 'Someone has to stay behind to clean up the Golden Horn. Do think those fishermen on the Galata Bridge would be there without me?'

'So you're an expert in pollution?', Nurettin remained standing.

'I wouldn't say I'm an expert in anything. How we would all want to be that'. He resisted Nurettin's precociousness. In fact, just one glance at his in-tray betrayed the feeling that this particular file had 'Do Not Approve' stamped all over it. He'd thought this from the moment the file reached his desk, but reluctantly he had to go through with this interview. He didn't want to give any other information to Nurettin than he had prepared, so he opened the file and started while Nurettin reluctantly sat down.

'Turkey, Syria and Iraq are all starting to suffer the effects of global warming. There has been less rain and as a result water levels in the dams, particularly the Atatürk dam, are decreasing year-on-year. You know we have faced criticism from Iraq over our dam construction programme over the years. But Turkey has been very far sighted with the GAP project, it was a huge development programme for our country. The Euphrates is the only reliable source of running water for Syria. You recall that President Tulonel said that Syria and Iraq have no better claim to Turkey's rivers than Ankara does to their oil and Turkey has the right to do anything it likes with its water resources.'

'Can I stop you there? I am not here for a lecture'.

'Let me continue, then you can say something'. The technician lifted up his head from his papers. Nurettin gave him a disapproving look.

'On various occasions......', the technician started again. Nurettin began to gaze at the picture of Atatürk on the wall behind this low ranking government official. Nurettin wondered what the

151

founder of modern Turkey would have made of men in the twenty-first century paying money to have cosmetic surgery for a moustache implant.

The official continued '....Syria has claimed that it had acquired rights over the Euphrates and Tigris rivers dating back to ancient times. It would like to have a share of the water from these rivers on a mathematical basis. Nevertheless, Turkey has sacrificed energy generation to relieve Iraq and Syria from shortages of water'.

Nurettin interrupted, 'Syria has had their own problems with the design and construction of some of their dams, that's why their power generation has been so poor; they have salinization caused by over-pumping and collapse of canals due to seepage'.

'Well, to an extent that's true, the Euphrates basin soils are in large part gypsiferous, prone to erosion and so suitable only for careful applications of irrigation water'.

'That's my point - to what extent can Turkey be held responsible for mistakes that the Syrian government has made? Turkey can't be blamed for the geological conditions of the Euphrates on the Syrian side of the border'.

'So, you want to punish them for that?'

'No, I'm not proposing to punish them. You touched on it earlier. There will be a mathematical basis for charging them. I have prepared those models. You've studied them, I hope?'

'I'm going to study them more fully'.

'When?'

'Let me finish please. Your case is quite aligned with some of my colleagues thinking. But the commercialisation of the operation is quite problematic – suggesting that these management fees are extracted as compensation for your idea'.

'Think of it as intellectual property'.

'We can come back to you within two weeks to tell you whether we can help with this or not.'

'There's nothing else I can say to convince you now?'

'No, I think we're finished here'. Nurettin left the room, the building and skipped down the stairs. He felt immediately exposed to some form of ozone pollution and began to rub his left eye. He recalled the previous evening when in Kartakoy he'd seen a remarkable orange sunset, not as deep orange and red as the ones you see in West Texas, but spectacular all the same. That was industrial pollution.

Nurettin picked up a yellow cab which drove him all the way to the Anatolian side down to the Turkish Naval Academy in Tuzla. He'd managed to arrange a meeting with a military official. He arrived there just before lunchtime.

There was certainly going to be a time when the military would not be involved in government once the Welfare Party increased in popularity. That time had not yet come so there was an opportunity to do this.

Once through security, where the contents of his case were checked, he was ushered into a spacious, airy room with plenty of natural light. The only document he was carrying with him was his thesis which was of no particular interest to the naval guard.

As the military official stepped out from behind his desk, Nurettin noticed he was of medium height, wore braces, a shirt without a tie, and scruffy trousers indicating he might have slept in them. Presumably the military uniform had been discarded earlier in the day, although Nurettin saw no sign of it, neither on the back of his seat or behind the door. The two men sat down either side of the desk. This didn't feel like the power centre of the Kemalist military that used to shape the political landscape of the country. Nevertheless Nurettin was warmly welcomed. He suspected this might be an unusual event, such was the man's willingness to talk, even if he was telling Nurettin things he already knew.

'It would be fanciful to suppose', the military official spoke quietly and methodically, leaning over towards Nurettin as if to treat him in his confidence, 'that we could ever guarantee to supply Syria with 500 cubic metres of water per second from the

Euphrates'. He was referring to the agreement that Ankara had signed with Damascus. 'There is no way that the Turkish energy minister could increase the amount. If we are not careful there will be insufficient supply for us to generate electricity in the power plant in the Atatürk Dam! Now that would be a calamity'. The official sat back in his chair as if to reflect that Nurettin's proposal was small beer in comparison.

'We have to protect the people of south-eastern Anatolia, after all this is why we constructed the Dam. To provide water for irrigation and for hydroelectric plants to bring this area out of poverty'. His voice faded away to almost an inaudible level. From the edge of the desk, Nurettin noticed how small the man's feet were and he appeared to be wearing women's flat velvet shoes or else very fetching slippers.

'Iraq repeatedly says that we are holding back water despite good levels of rain and snow in the region of Euphrates on Turkish territory, but of course our government has denied that and will continue to deny it!', with fresh impetus, he carried on after a stutter and then a cough.

'Yes, but look at how much water the Iraqis are already losing under the Mosul dam', Nurettin raised the decibel levels.

'This is what happens when you build a dam on gypsum and anhydrite', the military official despaired with a shrug of his shoulders and a look through the window into the distance.

'Their machines for grouting have been stolen or damaged, they have insufficient supplies of cement. Are they really going to spend 250 million dollars with that Italian firm to reinforce and maintain the dam?, Nurettin interjected.

'If the dam fails, the water will arrive in Mosul in four hours', the military official said morosely.

'It will be in Baghdad in a couple of days after that', Nurettin volunteered loudly and pragmatically. Leaning forward 'so *we* can manage the risk for them by controlling supply further up the Tigris.' And, as if he was a pugilist, delivering another body blow, 'And charging them for it!' he shouted.

'Are you trying to play God?' the military official stood up. 'I think you had better leave'.

'No, listen,' Nurettin still seated, his voice deepening in a threatening way. He caught sight of two bow ties in a large ashtray on the desk. 'While Syria claims that it has increased the amount it has passed on to Iraq to make up for Turkey's shortfall, I find that hard to believe'.

The military official was unmoved and just stood and stared disapprovingly at Nurettin.

'It would be in the national interest' and then, for effect, Nurettin looked up at the colour portrait of Atatürk behind the military official's desk; he felt

156

the piercing blue eyes searching for him and his thoughts turned back to his schooldays, wondering whether he was following the correct strand of secularism that Atatürk had prescribed. From an early age this was always his excuse for not attending the mosque.

'Your ideas are totally at odds with Turkey's leniency towards its neighbours. Now go.' The military official sat down and snatched some paperwork across his desk towards him and began reading it. Nurettin pondered for a moment which faction of national security did his adversary represent. Then he stood up and left the office feeling that the encounter had been a marginal success. Whether he had been talking to the correct person was another matter.

A third meeting that day in the late afternoon was back in Levent, with a representative of a regional development bank. 'We are seen as the bad boys...... the modern day equivalent of asset strippers. But we'll persuade someone else to put their money behind you if you have a good idea.' It was clear that Cengiz hadn't read Nurettin's proposal.

'Can I ask how did you finance the bail-out of the pro-Government loss-making media agency?'.

'You really don't expect me to answer that'.

'Can you give me back the documents I sent you, then?'

Cengiz reached down into his desk drawer and pulled out the large envelope that Nurettin recalled sending.

At least in the early evening Nurettin had acceded to Jeder's request to meet him in Levent for dinner. Jeder had only just arrived when a black Audi drew up outside Tike's, and Nurettin climbed out. One of the two doormen was spurred into action and a boy was summoned to take care of the valet parking. Nurettin held the driver's door open for the boy, who climbed in and quickly drove off. The car disappeared from view, apparently on the way towards Bebek, but Nurettin had no doubt it would be there waiting for him when it came time to leave.

Quickly established at Jeder's table, Nurettin raised his shot of vodka, lime juice and crushed ice to give a toast, 'although it hurts me to say it', Nurettin laughed, 'thank you Mr. Papandreou'.

He carried on 'now even the Germans, with all their legions of guest workers, having hidden behind the Greek 'no' vote for so long, had to finally come out of the closet and come up with a good reason for keeping Turkey out'.

'Yes', said Jeder, 'but isn't it all about the burden of the funding of 80 million, mostly poor, population or is it the faith?'

'It's been more than one nation blocking it for so long', Jeder added, trying to douse Nurettin's hopes a little. 'Remember it's not just Munich but also Milan and Manchester, take your pick'.

'Hey, you guys have the Christian Democratic Party, why can't you accept the Islamic Democratic Party', Nurettin was more convinced than Jeder.

'Here are you plotting water wars and I am simply trying to grow rice in Trabzon and ship olive oil to the rest of the world. There are many more commodities unexploited in this country of yours, why foul it up for everybody else by messing with the water?'

Nurettin was late returning to his street in Nişantaşı. He half expected Aruş to be lurking in the shadows of the poorly lit street with a gun bought with the proceeds from that morning; someone had to stick up for Şişko, Tunç and all the others. Nurettin hadn't come up with the money he'd promised the others in the previous week. The Ponzi scheme really had fallen apart; without Jeder's contribution there would be no more money coming in.

When he reached his apartment block there were several letters at the bottom of the stone stairs inside the front door. The best quality white envelope had Tulon Holdings' logo franked in bold print above his name and address. He opened the envelope carefully as if he didn't want to rip a money order inside. It was a formal letter signed by Hussein Yıldırım above his printed name and full title. 'We have decided to support your scheme' was all that Nurettin needed to read.

8

PROMISE YOU GAVE

Jeder was at the end of his year's travel budget even though it was only the end of October. The mud was still caked and wet on his boots from his trip to Trabzon but now he needed to go away again and at that moment the only restriction on his travelling was the lack of budget.

On Tuesday morning when Jeder arrived at the office a little late Azize was already at her desk, her door to Mehmet's office was open so Mehmet was already there too. Jeder knocked firmly and put his head around Mehmet's office door, he couldn't contain his curiosity any longer.

'*Ne istiyorsunuz*?', Mehmet thought it must be Jeder because for most other people Azize would have entered his room first to check whether he was available to see someone without an appointment. Mehmet kept his head down, checking some reports. He looked up. He was immaculately presented, Jeder less so, Mehmet looked him up and down with disdain.

'What happened', Jeder smiled in attempt to remove Mehmet's scowl.

'The trial has been delayed. And...' a semblance of a smile came across Mehmet's face indicating his satisfaction that such a demand could ever have been accepted, 'I managed to secure a request for anonymity for all my staff in the period leading up to any trial. It wasn't easy but I thought it was important for us to have some protection while we find out what really is happening here'.

'Well, that's good', there must be a catch. 'Falsified evidence? Did that buy us some time?'

'Sit down, there's something else I need to discuss with you. It's the *rice* project', Mehmet hesitated over the word 'rice' as if incredulous that he was saying it. 'Your trip reports always read like travel guides. I know you like this country but remember that the readers of your reports are nearly always Turkish people, most of whom know their country in a different way than you'.

Mehmet continued, 'I go back to what I said to you when you arrived, Australian average yields of 9 metric tonnes per hectare are well beyond our reach, and for all rice producing countries around the world, global warming is working against us rather than for us.

We had to attract western capital. Add this to Turkish entrepreneurship. First, we had to secure land. Ankara has been good enough to help us to do that. Look at how many countries have failed rice projects. People continually underestimate start-up costs'. And, as if Jeder's earlier intended quip about evidence had given Mehmet the impetus he needed, 'now, I am cutting off the supply of cash. Yıldırım has decreed it. The payback is too uncertain and too long term.'

As Mehmet saw Jeder about to protest: 'Yıldırım has heard of projects failing in Brazil and Nigeria.' It was necessary to keep talking to stop Jeder saying anything.' We cannot afford to keep pumping in capital into a project that does not have scale nor looks like ever having it.'

Jeder stood up: 'We were going to structure this to provide gains to smallholders who were willing to take the risk and with their hard work they would see the reward. Hakan has already identified plenty of suitable candidates.'

'Yes, but none of them has signed up', Jeder was surprised that Hakan must have told Mehmet this information.

'The concept of using drip irrigation systems to allow for all year round farming is a good one. The water is delivered directly to the roots maximizing plant growth and improves yields.' Jeder continued 'Ankara was about to grant us a long term lease for a large amount of fertile land. We cannot back out now.'

'I've told you, and that's the decision'.

'I need to go for one more trip to convince you'.

'If you miss your targets this month I am going to have to fire you', Mehmet shouted this with a half smile that quickly disappeared. It wasn't a joke. 'At least leave Hakan here so that business doesn't stop completely'.

Jeder felt that if he turned up to confront the farmers without Hakan he wouldn't be taken seriously; an Englishman on his own purporting to represent Turkey in this kind of technical arena just wouldn't work.

'You're just a tourist, go away!' was Mehmet's last shot as Jeder left his office.

There was no sign that Hakan had returned to their office since their trip to Trabzon or else he'd been particularly meticulous at covering his tracks. Jeder even checked the back of the door to see if Hakan had brought back his coat but he hadn't. Maybe he was really sick, in which case Jeder wondered whether he was going to be at the airport the following day. Gathering his own coat, more because he felt he wouldn't return to the office for a while rather than thinking he was actually going to wear it, the Trabzon rice project file and his diary, Jeder walked out of the office.

That evening Jeder finally made contact with Gail. He had been calling several nights during the week and had expected one of his sons to pick up, if not Gail herself. When she answered she sounded bright and happy with no hint of a cloud of five years' history of putting up with ˙ Jeder's self-centredness. 'So what is the progress on the job?', she asked.

'I'm leaving for Almaty a week on Sunday'.

'So, you won't be coming back to England from Istanbul before you go to Almaty? You are leaving, lock stock and barrel?'

Gail changed tack, 'do you know what one of the mothers said to me today at school?: 'Why don't you have a baby of your own?' I was mad but this time I didn't say anything. I don't feel the need to explain my way out of other people's prejudices. I wonder what they say about me at home. Maybe they think I am profiteering out of the boys, I am having something for nothing, didn't have to be married, didn't go through pregnancy and childbirth, and didn't have to divorce. They conveniently ignore the fact that I'm the only adult in the house. I am the lynchpin of the household, you are absent and irresponsible, unreliable. I could suffer from depression. I could need help'. This all felt a world away for Jeder.

'Do you know', Gail continued, 'the boys are always being told by the other kids that both their parents are dead, or that their father is useless and their mother is in an asylum?'

Gail was looking at her choices and each telephone call there was a chance she might say he could have his boys back.

'Sometimes it's easier for me to say that the boys' parents are dead, then their whole perspective of me changes. Little do they know that there is not only one parent still alive but also one who is at least capable. Other times I say the boys know who their father is, they know where he is and they know that he loves them. I can give them everything else they need.' Jeder was just waiting for her to say 'Have the boys back, you need to take them back now'.

'Just wait a minute, there is somebody at the door'.

'You don't want to hear about your sons!?', Gail's tone became urgent but her voice became fainter as he dropped the handset and he rushed to catch the door. Jeder only heard the first two words, 'Mr. Edwards?', but he knew what the rest of the sentence was going to be.

Two uniformed policemen were at the door. One of them handed him a clipboard which was a restriction order. Jeder's Turkish was just about good enough to understand he was about to be taken into custody for questioning and he would no longer be allowed to stay in his house. Jeder recalled Nurettin's warnings about being civil towards the police, 'We still have state security courts, remember that,....and torture'. Jeder had dismissed this as an over-reaction after Nurettin had returned, frustrated, from one of his visits to the military; this was 2002 after all.

After a minute of hesitation, the officers judged this was enough time for him to have digested the entire contents of the order, even though Jeder had only made it through the first paragraph. Jeder let the officers in and he understood that they wanted him to pack a suitcase of clothes and belongings. One of them remained downstairs looking around, replacing the phone handset in its holder, the other came up to his bedroom with him.

'How long should I pack for?'

'About a week, maybe longer. You'll need your passport', and, as soon as Jeder had located it, the officer took it from him.

'When will I have it back?'

'Most probably you'll have to attend court in a week'.

'Where are you taking me now?'

'Hurry up, please'.

He thought about what clothes he needed and took down a small case from the top of the wardrobe. He searched for some folders, pamphlets and some loose papers on his table to put into a second packing case. He could see the police officer starting to lose patience with him and he called downstairs to his colleague.

The second man came upstairs, 'I need access to your loft'.

'My loft'.

'Yes, where is the entrance?'

Jeder went out onto the landing and pointed to the loft door and the collapsible ladder. The second man went up quickly as if this was an act he performed regularly and began walking around inside the loft space.

'There's no time for that.....you won't need all of these'. Jeder returned to his bedroom and saw that the first man had selected two of his work files apparently at random. He heard the officer in the loft have a short mobile telephone conversation with someone else, as if he was organising a vehicle to be brought around to the front of the house in readiness for Jeder's exit. The policemen certainly didn't appear to expect Jeder to be obstructive, there were no handcuffs.

As he was being gently led out of his house by the police officers, they were joined by two plain-clothed or security officers, one of whom took the two cases from him. He didn't expect to see the case with the two work files again. The other security officer asked him to stand still and straight while he rolled up his trouser leg and fitted a tagging device.

Once done, the first security officer read in English from another sheet fixed to the same clipboard 'You'll need permission to go anywhere, your purpose will need to be verified. You can't use a car, you have to take public transport, taxi or a *dolmuş*. Your telephone calls will be recorded'. That was a lot more latitude than Jeder expected.

'Am I going to be staying in police barracks?' The police officer shrugged his shoulders, either Jeder's Turkish was unintelligible or conversation was prohibited, although at no time did he give the impression that Jeder was an inconvenience or a burden, more of an experiment.

Not all the police officers left the house and he left without his keys. For sure they would be scouring his house for cash but they wouldn't find any, even in the loft. In the van Jeder started to read the clipboard order but couldn't understand the nature of the suspected offence that he had committed. He tried to work out who of his work colleagues, finding him an unnecessary irritation, could have schemed his confinement, just as he believed he was about to move further east. Perhaps Emin had known all along, or maybe Mehmet found something that Jeder had overlooked and had forced Hakan to corroborate.

As he was removed from his house, Jeder consigned all plans to the dustbin. These included a token snapshot of how his life in Istanbul could have been, an idyll that had him inventing a childhood in Istanbul. At Emirgan, going down to the water, gazing out over the Bosphorous towards Paşabahçe on the Asian side; jumping on the small boat leaving from Yenikoy for the crossing to Beykoz, searching for walnuts and figs.

In the van one of the plain clothed officers reassured him in English, 'Don't worry, there will be a judicial process. There will not be police interference in the court hearing'. To his surprise the police van dropped him out at small backstreet hotel in Beyoğlu. He didn't need to check in, this was done by one of the police officers; he was given a room number and walked up two flights of stairs with his bags unaccompanied by any officer. As soon as he reached the hotel room he slumped on the bed without changing or washing. He checked the phone, it was live, so it seemed he had the ability to make outside calls.

Jeder thought he was in a deep sleep and it must have been after midnight but something woke him. It was a helicopter overhead. He rushed to the hotel room window but couldn't see anything but the building a few metres opposite. It must have been directly overhead. The whirring sound abated and he went back to bed but as soon as he was lying down the helicopter came back. This circular pattern which took about two minutes to run its course, was repeated over the next twenty minutes or so with the volume increasing and then reducing, whining like a persistent mosquito which, even if he put all the lights on and was poised like a coiled spring with his rolled up newspaper, he was unable to extinguish.

Then the hotel room phone rang. It was Nurettin.

'Did you think that nobody would notice you were concocting records of shipments of oil at preposterous volumes and prices?' Jeder wasn't surprised Nurettin knew where to find him, nor by his burgeoning English vocabulary. Jeder began to resent his English Literature teacher at Manchester Grammar for failing to inspire him to read more. Nurettin's baritone was a little more cracked than usual implying a head cold. Jeder didn't think a reply was required.

'You are producing the wrong sort of oil'. Nurettin spoke as if he was reading from a prepared statement, which was unusual for him.

'You will not be allowed to tamper with any evidence', he continued like an automaton. Jeder was waiting for an offer for a meal at a restaurant.

'With no ties to Turkey you have significant incentive and ability to flee', the recorded message continued. Jeder moved over to the window, stretching in vain to see anything to look at in the dark other than the dimly lit wall opposite. Going east for a change of name, change of identity, a new city and a new town. A new identity and a new job in a new town. That plan could also be binned.

'The more you show to people that you are normal the more anyone who knew you from before will want to know how you could have acted at another level'.

'Jeder, you are there?' the authentic Nurettin assumed control.' Did you already eat something?'

'There's no room service here', Jeder checked the hotel brochure. 'Why don't you come here?'

'I heard about your abduction from the house. Do you really think they'd let me into the hotel?'

'Well they've let you call me! They obviously know who you are!'

'Hey, don't cut off the hand that feeds you'.

'I thought I was feeding you – would you mind if the money stops?'

'Why should it?'

'Oh, because I thought you were about to tell me that I have become a liability and that we should sever relations'.

'I'd heard you were leaving for Almaty?'

'With this tag around my ankle? Fat chance.'

'There's no case yet, why do you think they have allowed you to be cooped up in a hotel instead of in a cell, there's no case to prove'.

'I think I need to go out', Jeder put the phone down.

Jeder wasn't to know it but the tagging system was not yet in operation so it was not recorded that he left his hotel room nor when he walked straight through the hotel foyer and out into the street.

9

CONQUERED

The first detailed meeting with the Tulon people was in an unused retail space in Akmerkez. The room wasn't heated and already in November Nurettin's hands were feeling the cold. He'd half expected to meet in Yıldırım's lush offices in Levent, but the terse message left on his answerphone directed him here. Before he'd left home that morning Arzu had told him not to risk throwing it all away. He replied saying he wasn't going to throw anything away.

The Tulon representative went straight to the point about the area that would be affected by the impact of supply control from Turkey.

'The local people there say that it's the Syrian government that controls their water supply, and who is responsible for charging them these high rates. They say that whatever the cost of water that is transferred from Turkey, the Syrian government will double it. Then the Syrian government will blame that on the Turks'. He continued, 'it's not a great place. Mosquitoes thrive in the fetid pools along the river. The soil is full of salt. The biggest problem is water – bad water everywhere. There is an absence of the snow-melt irrigation systems feeding water from the hill slopes to support food crops, livestock and orchards; there were some but these have not been maintained. Some of these could still be repaired, others need to be completely rebuilt. The trouble is the sewage goes into the canal ditches, which are used for washing, cooking and drinking.

In the area we are talking about there are perhaps 600 births a year in a community of 21,000. Of these, 30% will die between the age of 10 days and one month. And at least 10% of the 600 mothers will die in childbirth every year. It's a problem of food and water - the mothers are just unable to sustain the babies. Part of the problem is that there are no midwives and men will not let their wives and daughters be treated by male doctors and nurses.

Women are hidden from view, you may see the odd nomad in a black burkha. Young girls of 13 are traded for bride prices of up to US$ 20,000. The buyers are typically men in their forties or older. These men are gangsters, middlemen or gang warlords. It is not uncommon in remote compounds to see women and girls in appalling conditions, some with noses missing and others with ulcers on their necks. Building a clinic staffed with midwives and female doctors is a small step in the right direction. Conflict resolution is usually about stopping one farmer hitting another with a spade in a dispute about water rights. What do you think of all that?'

'As you say, it's not a great place to start with'. Nurettin's physical actions contradicted his private impulses. Any philanthropic or charitable tendencies were squashed by his continued plotting for monetary gain and self-aggrandizement.

'These are the people whose livelihoods your scheme will threaten'.

'My scheme? I thought we were in this together?'

'Imagine if you were to meet these people. They're being hurt by your punitive water rate'.

'When is that likely to occur? When am I ever likely to see them?'

This question remained unanswered. The Tulon people didn't appear to have the same level of enthusiasm as was conveyed in Yıldırım's letter, but Nurettin pressed on. He'd already received the first two payments from them.

'There's always the potential to extend this scheme,' Nurettin thought it was time to push on. 'Other rivers, you know'.

'I don't think that's something we want to talk about at the moment'.

'The Tigris', just in case the penny hadn't dropped. That was pretty much the end of the meeting, Nurettin had arranged another trip to

Madrid and needed to cut short any further discussion to reach the airport on time.

Javier was at home in Majadahonda preparing for Nurettin's visit. Documents and maps lay strewn all over the dining room table at his rented house off the A6 on the outskirts of Madrid. He cast his gaze over the maps of the Guadiana River Basin and pored over all the reports he could find about how the Spanish authorities regulated the flow downstream. He pondered over whether this was the correct blueprint for Nurettin's requirements. He asked himself again whether he really wanted to be involved in this Turkish project. Once in, he thought, '*de donde no se vuelve.*'

It took Nurettin quite a while to reach Majadahonda from the airport but, once there, he was in an ebullient mood when Javier greeted him at his door.

'I have some great news! My wife is pregnant. Already 9 weeks!'

'What a thrill and what a gift to be pregnant…again! I am waiting for that child, unborn and unnamed!'

'No, this would be the first'.

'So, we must celebrate, come in. No need to take off your shoes'. Javier realised that he didn't have any champagne in the house but he had a magnum of Ribera del Duero that he had been wanting to find an excuse to open for some time.

'Yes, but let's do that later, let's have a look at this first'. Nurettin had already gravitated towards the dining room with its assorted paraphernalia.

He congratulated Javier on his research and preparation. 'The dam and reservoir construction you are illustrating here is exactly in line with what is being discussed by the Turkish government and a large private conglomerate with whom I am in discussion'.

'You see here,' Javier pointed to an area on one of his maps, but Nurettin didn't look at but just looked at Javier instead. 'In this basin, over 90% of water was used for irrigation. There is already an established water pricing policy both for agricultural and residential consumption'

'Perfect', Nurettin pulled the heavy table closer to him, destabilizing Javier, whose elbow had been resting on the edge of the table. 'I have never had so much control. No drinking water for 48 hours will mean widespread livestock loss, which will also in turn affect the price of food. Think about it.... no dates, no wheat, no barley, no rice... and more, terrible, dust storms. That's in all the poor areas'.

'What about the rich areas?', Javier stood up straight to face Nurettin. 'Every day in urbanisations people expect to be able use more water than before, three or four times the usage of their parents' generation.'

'But not all countries have coastline developments like you have in your country and Portugal; where they need more water for their gardens, their swimming pools and their golf courses.'

'Yes, but in your country and *my country*, there is no premium charged for the water that is used in the swimming pool over the water that is being used for people to clean their hands', Javier emphasised 'my country' as he took exception to the way Nurettin had suddenly assumed so much knowledge about Spain. Some of the earlier bonhomie surrounding the announcement about a baby was beginning to dissipate. Before any ground was going to be given, Javier wanted to construct his own ringed fence around it, and electrify it. After all, Nurettin was in Javier's house and was already criticising the way his country was governed, even though he agreed.

'Most countries consider that water for washing, cooking and sanitation is a basic human right. There are huge variances between how countries charge their citizens and their businesses for water usage. These variances are amplified when one country charges its neighbour. It's a commodity in an imperfect market. Where there are such huge pricing imperfections there are huge opportunities, it's a question of how to corner the supply,' Nurettin stared at Javier awaiting his reply.

'Globally, there is too much water used for agriculture, not enough money is being applied to fix pipe leaks or extend the pipes to reach more homes. We are a long way from addressing the imbalance between agricultural water usage and domestic consumption. You must have seen how agricultural productivity can be improved in your trips with Mario,' Javier suddenly remembered all Nurettin's helicopter trips.

Nurettin stretched out on the only comfortable chair in the room, 'Then, with control over the water supply, I can flood the dry rivers at will. When a river is flooded, the topography of that river bed is altered, the behaviour of the river changes.'

'Not all water use is a basic human right, why should you be allowed to flood dry river beds?'

There was no need to answer that, so Nurettin just said 'nine billion mouths to feed by 2050. Just imagine the pressure on resources, food and water supply.'

'So, what about Jeder, is he guilty?'

'I really don't know'.

'¡Sin dudas!'

'And what about his family? Surely someone knows something? What about accomplices?'

'That's not clear either'

'Sus familiares expresaron dudas de que el solo fuera capaz de cometer semejante crimen por cuenta propia'.

'That may be so. That may be'. Nurettin didn't want Javier's surmise to fester.

Nurettin had expected so much from this trip to Spain. Especially as now Jeder had become to feel like a little piece of grit in Nurettin's boot. This tiny piece of dirt translated into a large stone underneath his sock, constantly reminding him of its presence on each footfall, uncomfortable and destabilising.

'It takes me too long to come all the way out here, can we meet in the Retiro next time?', Nurettin was leaving Majadahonda a lot happier than when he arrived.

'It'll be cold in the park next time you come. Send my best wishes to your wife'. Javier concluded that Nurettin didn't drink; his Ribera remained uncorked.

Javier began to think about his obituary. He liked the sound of 'engineer and architect, as well as sculptor and painter', like one of Valencia's more famous sons. But, unlike Calatrava, Javier didn't have a plan of how to achieve that and, at thirty-seven, he was a little bereft of ideas and running out of time. Maybe after all he should have pursued a career as a stand-up comic or a ventriloquist; that way, he could have seen his name in the papers for the right reasons.

1 0

CAUGHT COAT

Nurettin skulked outside the back street door, like a kid frustrated that his best friend's mother had just told him that his friend would not be coming out to play that day, under any conditions; without revealing exactly which rule had been broken, the vehemence of the mother's communication was going to leave Nurettin brooding outside the door knowing that his friend had no conventional escape route.

He'd rather have been on the top floor of a five star hotel in the smart Beşiktaş district, but Nurettin was in a Beyoğlu back street standing outside a service duct from the basement of a two star hotel. The building he'd been directed to was next to the hotel.

Nurettin stood on tip toes and then on the second clip of the drainpipe trying to see through the window, but the glass of the cloakroom was cloudy, and that was not the room in which Jeder was being detained. Nurettin couldn't even have seen if he was being punished.

Maybe circumstances had changed; he didn't want to play with Nurettin anymore and his mother was providing a formidable screen between Nurettin and the truth. Perhaps his best friend's mother didn't like the look of Nurettin, thought he might lead Jeder astray and was discouraging her son from further contact. Nurettin felt he would still have ample opportunities at school, away from the shield of his best friend's mother, to cultivate the friendship of his mate. These types of transformations had happened before, so Nurettin was used to the disappointment but would not be disheartened.

To the frustration of Nurettin, opening time of this police checkpoint building was twenty minutes later than scheduled, meaning for certain there would be twenty minutes less time available. No extension to this visiting period was granted.

There was quite a crowd building and it became evident that if Nurettin did not lead the way then others would. When the service door was eventually opened, people shoved and barged their way ahead of Nurettin and then on through the gap between the tall, thick doors and the corpulent guards. Nurettin was unbalanced by the rush and the belt on his coat caught the latch on one of the doors on the way through, halting his progress further until he disentangled himself.

It took a further half hour for any progress. After waiting in a tiny, sweaty cloakroom for his turn, Nurettin was ushered through three briefing rooms each containing a total of ten minutes or so of questioning from successively higher ranked officers. Or was the sequence policeman, prison governor to a lawyer representing the state? For a suspect who was being detained for an alleged price fixing charge, this seemed to be an overkill, but no doubt the officers were much more interested in Nurettin than they were with Jeder. For a time, the questioning puffed up Nurettin's self-importance, giving him an opportunity to expound on his achievements, real or imagined. Anyway, he held the upper hand in the discussions as if it was an extended tennis clay court rally; at some point he would end the tussle with a decisive shot which his opponents could not reach.

Two years previously when colleagues from the Paris office had taken him for a day to Roland Garros, and he had marvelled at the sparring of the players on the *terre battu,* impressed more by their mental strength than their amazing physical condition. The players who were thirty-seven were not the ones winning Roland Garros, but the ones who were still twenty-nine were! How early were life's opportunities restricted! Furthermore, those in their twenties who were the champions probably began playing serious tennis at four years old. Now even more conscious that he was pushing thirty he recalled that stamina was another impressive ingredient for success as, after a while, the repetitions of the questioning and the officers' increasingly harassed tone began to unsettle him as he regularly checked the time on his wrist watch.

Eventually he was allowed through into the room with Jeder and two guards. The room was tiny, containing a bed, a table and two chairs and an old wardrobe. Probably where originally there was one room, now there were four, but at least in this one there was one window with a strong shaft of light. Jeder was wearing light nondescript trousers, a cream t-shirt and old trainers. He didn't react when Nurettin entered the room. Nurettin had the impression that Jeder's sleep the previous night had been, at best, fitful, and that he could have been in this room for some time as he had dozed off, with his face just about supported by his arm at the edge of the bed, his eyes closed.

Nurettin stood over Jeder. The obstructing and then the revealing of the light by his movements awoke Jeder from his doze. His eyelids moved although not perfectly synchronised, as if there was more glue on the left eye than the right one. Nurettin moved closer and smelt Jeder's damp and oily skin, and then recoiled as if he had seen an insect crawling up his neck.

'When you're sleeping you have the face of a wolf....and the breast of a chicken! Who were your parents and how is your family? One of your parents must have been Turkish...no?' Nurettin moved closer to Jeder and began to shout as if somehow this period of seclusion had impaired his hearing. 'One of your parents must have been Turkish, I said'.

'Did you un-holster your gun at the reception?' Jeder released his chin from the palm of his right hand and engaged eye contact. Jeder shouldn't have been surprised by how healthy and smart Nurettin appeared.

'This is not Trabzon'.

'You haven´t brought the stiff-necked man with you?', Jeder retorted as he shifted his weight onto his backside and tried to sit up with a straight back which was difficult because he was on the edge of the bed away from the wall.

Nurettin surveyed the room, surprised by its relative opulence. 'So this is your gilded cage. Normally people on corruption charges are put in jail. At least I expected three of you in one room, why do you have special treatment?'

'There's nowhere to walk around', Jeder's back was still bent so it was easier to look at the floor rather than at Nurettin. 'They're saying that I'm held under the state of emergency laws'.

'*What* state of emergency?' apart from Cyprus blowing up again, Turkish politics was quiet as far as Nurettin was concerned. There was as little state intervention as he could ever recall.

'Sending and receiving letters or any unsupervised communication is absolutely forbidden'.

'Have you spoken to Mehmet yet?'

'I don't need to. His company is not under investigation by Turkey's police or judiciary'.

'You're talking to me now.' Jeder didn't react to this.

Nurettin moved to sit at the table and hoped Jeder would follow him. Jeder appeared immobile so Nurettin continued standing up. 'From what I've told you about him, what would you do if you met Javier?'

'I'd go with him to Valencia...to look at the rice.'

'You know, unscrupulous rice hoarders face economic sabotage charges that carry a life sentence. I suppose you are the last person I need to talk to about price cartels or mislabelling of government-subsidized rice as a private brand?'

'Are you suggesting that I didn't mention on my labels that high fructose corn syrup was a contributory factor to America's obesity crisis and its growing diabetes rate?'

'How long do you have to talk today?', Nurettin wanted to move on to the subject he had come to talk about. The fact that he imagined he had sighted a rat scurrying down a long corridor before diving through a broken drain cover, when he arrived, made him feel uneasy he had to conduct business in these confined quarters.

'What, so God has really sent you to proclaim release for the captives? If you are interested then, one thousand, eight hundred and seventeen days....and that is if they don't set an example of me and extend it for another five years.'

'Do you really think I can wait that long?', Nurettin was beginning to wonder whether he was wasting his time.

'Don't worry, at least half the people here are HIV positive and the rest are dying of TB, so I probably won't make it.'

'You'd better be careful who you make friends with'.

'Every move has to be pre-determined, have you seen how cramped the common areas are?' Jeder said, knowing that Nurettin could not have seen them or even wanted to imagine them. It was not easy to make Nurettin uncomfortable, he saw only what he chose to see and ignored the rest. Jeder seized an opportunity as the two guards came together for a conversation turning their backs to Nurettin and Jeder. 'You must be missing my monthly contributions?'

'Not at all, I have several others like you, how do you think I have come so far?'

The guards turned back but clearly hadn't been listening. Nurettin was running out of time. If they allowed him another chance to see Jeder it would not be in this dungeon. They'd move him to another place in a few days.

'What about a lawyer?', Nurettin asked.

'Tulon has sent someone, he has already been twice. It's not really his field. He is going to find someone appropriate, he says'.

'But you will be moved somewhere else after the outcome of the trial'.

'Thanks', said Jeder.

'Just be careful when they allow you to play football with the other inmates that they don't beat you up'.

'What, for what I've done or for who I am?'

'Both, of course, but let me say what I have to say because there is not much time. We have suffered further setbacks,' Nurettin started. 'Yet again Brussels has suspended talks with Ankara. Again the EU is expecting Turkey to open up its ports and airports to the southern part of Cyprus. We have already included them in the customs union, what more is expected? You probably haven't heard about this. Changing the subject.... what is your strategy?'

'My strategy?', Jeder finally looked up.

'To survive, to come through unscathed?' Nurettin volunteered as Jeder paused for an answer.

'Only a fool would discuss a bribe in front of witnesses.'

Nurettin hesitated. He had never really thought of their financial arrangement involving a bribe. Although he was sure he could not be implicated, any money he had received from Jeder had not, in turn, been used to bribe anyone.

'But there are no incriminating documents, you assured me?' He knew the question wouldn't be answered as Jeder was now irritated to the point of silence by Nurettin's rhetorical style.

Nurettin cast his gaze around. The room really was a cubicle, conservatively hardly three metres square. It smelt of dead cats. With three people standing up, Nurettin was always close to one or other of the guards. Jeder, sitting down on his bed, was sandwiched between the table and the wall. Leaning slightly to his left, one of the guards made head and then eye contact with Nurettin and told him he had five more minutes, maximum, with Jeder.

'It was meant to be fifteen.' Nurettin moved to his left, making sure he didn't touch the other guard.

'You were late'.

'I've had three minutes so far'.

The guard shifted his gaze to Jeder, he certainly didn't need to continue speaking to Nurettin. Although this particular guard didn't speak English, Nurettin wasn't to know that. Even if either of the guards had understood, they had no idea which part of the conversation was code. Jeder thought back to Emin's remark - even if the guard spoke English and French he was probably disenamoured in his job and was just about to leave the service.

'Yes I had heard about it', Jeder retrieved the attention of Nurettin. 'You'd be surprised what we have access to here. It's not an impregnable fortress like Imralı here, but it is different. We have access to books. And of course I have a lot of time on my hands. A lot of thinking time; not a lot of reading time, the light is almost always poor. Since my glasses broke when they fell out of my trouser pocket onto the concrete floor and then I trod on one of the lens accidentally I haven't been able to have them repaired or replaced. So either I try very hard to read in one or two good hours of daylight when I am allowed or I rely on someone else. But that is nearly always unreliable information.'

'Stop making it sound like you have been here for ages, you're not in a cell, you haven't even been tried yet'.

'Thanks.'

'By rights, you should have been placed in a high-security prison. In these ones you are not allowed to commit suicide'.

'It's easier for someone to kill me in the hotel'.

'Let's continue, Europe is losing Turkey now,' said Nurettin. 'Once again, all we are being offered is this so-called 'privileged partnership' and nobody is going to buy that with the restrictions that come with it'.

'From memory, there are fewer than seventy Roman Catholic priests in Turkey, and that number is being reduced slowly. There are about 32,000 Catholics in the country.' Jeder wondered whether he had properly remembered that statistic, but left it.

'I think a more important fact is that we have been a member of Nato since 1952', Nurettin saw this conversation going nowhere. 'In addition I think as early as 1963 we were an associate member of the EEC.'

'Yes, but then you invaded Cyprus in 1974. It's in Europe and it's a holiday island. Think of all those EU commissioners who consider taking holidays there each year and wonder why they can't fly directly to the Northern part of the island'.

'When is it time for your football game?', this was the only exercise that Nurettin could recall Jeder taking before he was remanded in custody.

Jeder didn't answer but stared at Nurettin. Nurettin looked away. Now, he could smell dirty running water from outside. It was an uneasy proposition for Nurettin, water was being wasted. Yet it was dirty water, recyclable perhaps, but at an uneconomic cost and uneconomic to transport it to a region or a country where people could appreciate it or stay alive; eventually the sewer was the right place for it.

And just as for the first time that day Nurettin was actually thinking positively about his project, Jeder reflected on the undiscussed topic summarising all the negativity of Nurettin's plans, 'Do you want to build a road Nurettin, or be shot trying to blow one up?'

'I have complete faith in Turkey's judicial system. People know what is at stake in your case', Nurettin proclaimed.

Nurettin left. Jeder did go out later on the pretext of exercise and fresh air but his stiff back and bad mood precluded any involvement in physical activity.

The spectre of the Asilye Ceza courthouse hung over Jeder. It could have been worse, at least there was no accusation that Jeder had publicly denigrated the Turkish state, under Article 159. 'I'm looking at a six month suspended sentence, at worst', he thought as he struggled to shelter under an umbrella in the rain-swept five-a-side football cage at the back of the hotel, avoiding periodically having his legs taken from underneath him by two unbalanced players and a skidding ball.

The next day, when Jeder awoke, he tried to imagine the beautiful smell of a late March morning in the English countryside as spring approaches. It was difficult for him to analyse exactly what he thought he was missing. Once again, he faced the prospect of being taken before the criminal bench. Who would be his collaborators, his seasoned conspirators? Had their passports also been removed? At least he could be sure that the judges would have respect for the rule of law. For certain he would be given time to prepare his defence.

In the court hearing, the prosecuting lawyer began 'Are you Jeremy David Edwards?'

'Yes I am'.

This sitting was going to take twice as long as normal as the translator would repeat the lawyer's remarks sentence by sentence for Jeder's benefit in English.

He was already thinking about the judge's sentence. If he admitted to passing about US$ 150,000 in payments from an olive oil processor to his own third-party company then it would be three years in prison to be followed by two years in supervised release. In addition to the prison sentence, he would be ordered by the court to pay just under US$ 2 million in restitution to his former employer. Logically it followed that he wouldn't have a job anymore although nobody was saying this. The prosecutor stated:

'By accepting bribes in making his selling decisions, Jeremy Edwards defrauded his employer, his client and ultimately the Turkish consumer.'

'Mr. Edwards admitted helping Michael Lee Rearden, a broker and director at Cendar Foods, to charge their respective companies with inflated prices. For his part, Mr. Edwards ensured all necessary steps were in process to allow his company to sell approximately 35,000 tonnes of processed olive oil products to Cendar Foods at higher prices than usual between 2000 and 2001. Mr. Edwards pleaded guilty to two counts of fraud'.

'To be precise,' the prosecutor continued, "Mr. Edwards, 39, of Manchester, England, but currently living in Istanbul, pleaded guilty to two counts of depriving his company of his honest services by accepting US$ 158,000 in bribes to favour Cendar Foods when he sold the processed olive oil products".

'As part of the plea bargain, Mr. Edwards has admitted awarding Cendar Foods two contracts in May 2001 at prices lower than that of its competitors, causing his company to be denied of at least US$ 440,000 in receipts.'

'He also admitted that, in 2001, during a shortage of olive oil, he allowed Cendar Foods to essentially cancel its contractual obligation to buy 10,000 tonnes of olive oil at a set price. The revenue loss to Mr. Edwards' company was US$ 1.26 million'.

Giving evidence, the Head of Fraud Services commented 'We are aware that procurement fraud remains a problem and is an issue we see a great deal in our work; it is clearly unreported in comparison to our own experiences. What we have seen here is a classic case whereby a fraudster creates artificially high prices and transfers the differential to the real price to a third party bank account'. He concluded by saying 'the majority of procurement fraud is pretty uncomplicated and can be prevented by simple due diligence. This includes managers' awareness of employees' behaviour. Disgruntled employees as well as dishonest supervisors and managers can turn into fraudsters, with the two groups quite often colluding. Activity can begin with small amounts and then when the fraudster grows in confidence these misappropriated amounts will increase. Interestingly, in this case, the amounts defrauded have been consistent and similar in amount and frequency, making us believe that the defendant thought he could continue this activity for a long time with a monthly amount that was creeping under the radar'.

The prosecutor resumed 'Mr. Edwards is the first defendant to be sentenced as a result of the ongoing federal investigation into fraud and corruption in the olive oil industry. In a related case, two high profile purchasing executives of multinationals firms, whose names we are not at liberty to release at this time, have admitted to receiving illicit payments from Mr. Rearden and are awaiting sentencing. Mr. Rearden pleaded guilty on November 16th to racketeering, price fixing, bid rigging and contract conspiracies.'

To Jeder, the sums mentioned had been inflated, but not able to be contested. There seemed to be an open space where his defending attorney was meant to be sitting and now Jeder was powerless to complain. Had no one else noticed that these numbers didn't compute?

The judge addressed Jeder and the court room in a very sombre tone, 'In Turkey, our government is deemed to be only as strong as the strength with which it protects its own innocent citizens from law-breakers'. He went on, 'We have the legislation in place and the civil servants hired, to enforce the regulations, in order to prevent bad-intentioned people from robbing people of their belongings or taking away their rights. There is a perception here in Turkey that there are forces abroad that are involved in an effort to halt progress in this country. There are those abroad...and there are extensions of them within our country.' Then turning to Jeder specifically, 'In your particular sphere of expertise, Mr. Edwards, the buying and selling of commodities, trading is allowed.... but cheating is not.' He continued, not deviating from his stern expression, 'The path of those who expect results from financial misappropriation has been closed. Powerful and illicit circles within the business community whether emanating from outside or from within Turkey will be hounded out to ensure the bureaucratic and governmental institutions are not defrauded of tax revenues to which they are due. This trial will change the mentality of those who seek wealth and power without regard for the will of the people.'

Jeder was then conditionally released after the court hearing but ordered to remain in Istanbul, while his extradition request was considered. His only way out.

Jeder took a standard yellow city taxi to the airport at about 8.30 pm. At least he didn't have to worry about taking his passport. On the side of the back seat he had brought with him a small overnight bag containing two clean shirts, one pair of trousers, underwear, a toilet bag and two flimsy-back files. There was an on off-chance that, if his extradition had been approved, he wouldn't even be apprehended by police at the airport.

On the familiar unattractive route through the outskirts to the airport, Jeder revisited the same observations as when he first arrived in Istanbul.

There was a preference for concrete and a distinct absence of trees. Concrete appeared to mean progress but trees were considered old-fashioned and unprofitable. There was no planned building pattern, no conformity of height or width or colour co-ordination. All constructions - buildings was too generous a term - must have been put up in the previous five years. The airport vicinity sucked in small business gamblers, chancers, anybody scenting the possibility of diverting funds from part of a development grant by filling in a form, standing in a long queue on the pretext of operating a business near the new international airport expansion.

On the route, every now and then, there was a domestic dwelling with a concrete patio masquerading as a front garden. Occasionally, washing hung optimistically, still out there on a November evening. Where there was an opportunity for trees, bushes, hedges or flowers there was none. What trees there were had shed their leaves, there were not even any unattractive evergreens. In the harsh pollution from the traffic-laden road and the air turbulence that the trucks and *dolmuş* caused, Jeder reflected on what a challenge it must have been for those well-meaning planners, who had tried in vain to cultivate hedgerows at the side of the road. But trees... there were no excuses for not planting and cultivating more trees.

The taxi driver insisted on having the Fiat's heater on full, even though it wasn't a particularly cold November evening. Jeder asked him to shut it down, but instead he just switched up the radio louder. This forced Jeder to open the rear window for the last 15 minutes along the highway in the fast lane at 130 kph; the result was a stiff neck and an even more sore back from trying to manoeuvre himself into a position to avoid the direct blast of the wind, straining against an uncompromising seat belt. About as comfortable as a London cab, but considerably faster and at a fraction of the cost.

Jeder thought that perhaps he hadn't been effusive enough in his thanks for all Hakan had done for him; perhaps he was offended that Jeder hadn't gifted his car to him; instead, in trying to recoup some cash, Jeder had gone through a middle man who took the car off his hands and had found a Danish buyer to avoid him having to pay the foreigners' car purchase tax. Jeder never saw any of the agreed US$ 3,000 sale price and in fact ended up paying the middle man US$ 750 to fix the dashboard, have the car re-sprayed and valeted. Hakan could have done all that for him for a little less and then kept the car himself. Jeder doubted whether the car would ever reach the Dane but consoled himself that his car was too dangerous for Hakan. It was a monster, eight years old with at least 130,000 km on the clock, having endured a lifetime of shocks. It would be far too risky for Hakan to be driving Jeder's old car at night outside Istanbul, where trucks can drive fast along single carriageway roads and not always with their lights on.

When he reached the airport Jeder made for the Arrivals Hall rather than go to the check-in desks in Departures.

It couldn't have been the Hajj, that had surely happened earlier in the year, in February. It just seemed like half a million people were all returning from Mount Arafat in the middle of November. Large families with young kids were gathered to meet friends and relatives off the flight from Medina. For some reason all the travellers on domestic flights were arriving at the same terminal as those from international flights; some international flights had been delayed 3 to 5 hours, the ones from Africa had been delayed 12 hours, but the flights from Ankara, Izmir, Gazientep and Samsun were all due to arrive on time in the next hour.

The airport building was new; the workers still proud to be there, especially those new to their job, who involved themselves in the joy of families welcoming loved ones. At the same time these workers were still able to forgive the most delinquent visitor who didn't use a litter bin for his cigarette ash or a used copy of *Star* or *Hurriyet*. Jeder hadn't eaten since lunch but none of the airport offerings tempted him; only tired American-style take-away food at Western international airport prices; and these packages were handed over on the understanding from the seller that you must really have planned your day badly.

Jeder caught sight of Hakan's assistant waiting in the crowd for the incoming passengers. He was in his thirties, looked at least ten years older but Jeder couldn't believe he had a hard life. He was not proud and respectful as Jeder might have expected but instead, rather sheepish and hesitant. When Jeder approached him, Hakan's assistant looked like a rabbit caught in the headlights, giving Jeder a look as if he had wronged him in a past life and had the capacity to do so again. As Jeder gripped him by the hand his mousey eyes squinted as if it was painful or not appropriate, or both, for him to shake Jeder by the hand. Or, maybe Jeder's hands were dirty. As this acknowledgement was perfunctory, and Jeder did not want to immediately have his limited grasp of the language exposed, he quickly turned his attention to the target, the exit from the baggage reclaim, so as not to miss anyone.

From the waiting area in the Arrivals Hall, a procession of petty officials passed one way through the steel doors and into the baggage reclaim area. As the steel doors swung back into place so quickly it was very difficult to see exactly what was happening on the baggage reclaim side.

'I could do that', thought Jeder, 'it would save a lot of time'. Jeder had done that before when, arriving on an internal flight at Barcelona airport, he followed the wrong signs and surfaced at the taxi rank in the street, realising he had alighted at the incorrect baggage reclaim as he came out through the wrong terminal exit. He then needed to be escorted the wrong way through the steel doors to another terminal where he should find his baggage. The escort process petered out halfway as the attendant lost interest and Jeder almost emerged unchecked in the correct baggage reclaim. One of the guards, suspicious about what might be the contents in his overnight bag, stopped him but Jeder explained he had taken the wrong exit and needed to recover his main item of baggage. Jeder produced an old ticket stub from his overcoat pocket and waved it at the guard who had no chance to check it from that distance, but had no reason, on that day, to believe that Jeder was disingenuous. Maybe this happened a lot. Maybe it was that kind of day, following a union announcement about proposed industrial action that none of the airport staff felt unduly motivated, or felt fully confident about their ability to assess suspicious characters. But this official did ask Jeder to reveal the contents of his overnight bag. He was a little suspicious that the shirts appeared unworn and expertly pressed and that gave him increased confidence to stick to the protocol and denied him access.

Now at Atatürk International Airport in November 2002, Jeder needed to know that he was able to leave the country with impunity.

Jeder wondered for whom Hakan's assistant was waiting. His flight, like Jeder's, must have been delayed and as Jeder scanned the board, there were only four remaining incoming flights that should have arrived that evening, Ljubljana was delayed 17 hours and now scheduled to come in at 5.35am the next morning. That left direct flights from Frankfurt, Milan and London, all delayed between 2 and 6 hours. Jeder stared at the board. When there was no movement in two minutes watching, he began to convince himself that the airport staff had gone home, and there would be no further movement on the board until the morning. To move his mind off that thought and the image of the static board, it was time to take the plunge.

'Family?', Jeder asked.

'No, friends', came the reply.

'From Rome?', Jeder asked incredulously, as there was no Rome flight. He had completely misunderstood what Hakan's assistant was patiently trying to tell him.

'No, Frankfurt'.

'Late!', Jeder said, 'late, like the one I am waiting for from London'.

'Yes, God willing, the planes will not be delayed further'.

He offered Jeder a cigarette, even though smoking had been recently banned in public buildings. As people had begun to desert the terminal building and too many of the external sliding doors remained open to accommodate the myriad officials now leaving, it was chilly and Jeder accepted the offer, but their conversation had run out. He wanted to ask where Jeder's family was, but felt it impolite to intrude. Jeder, for his part, did not want to engage Hakan's assistant in further discussion about exactly what Hakan's assistant's friends did in Frankfurt, lest this dialogue would encourage Hakan's assistant to ask why Jeder was waiting at the airport at this time of night. To justify the reason to himself, and to try to give the impression to Hakan's assistant that the reason the conversation had momentarily ceased was that Jeder had to check some important information, Jeder rummaged in his jacket pocket.

Hakan's assistant was growing in confidence. Despite having accepted his hospitality of a cigarette, Jeder now walked off on the grounds of being too cold and needing to move around a bit to warm up or maybe see if there was anywhere still open in the building selling coffee or *cay* or a magazine to read.

Not that Jeder wanted to be kept awake. He leant on the restraining rail at the opposite side to Hakan's assistant and flicked through the pages of *Esquire*. Jeder could sense that Hakan's assistant was going to wait to see who were these friends of Jeder that were meant to arrive.

The Milan flight arrived, its passengers came and went and took more than half of the waiting crowd with them. After a while, Jeder thought he saw all the same passengers emerging through the steel doors who had just come through on the Milan flight. Or maybe there were just one or two people who went back through the steel doors with their baggage and then came out again. Surely one of Frankfurt and London flights had been cancelled.

Jeder checked the board again. The details had been updated, so there was still someone in the airport. For the dwindling crowd of people this information was important. The bad news was that, whilst the board confirmed that both the Frankfurt and London flights were still delayed, rather than cancelled, now the extra information defining the length of the delay had been scrubbed. Maybe there hadn't been any human intervention; after a prescribed time delay with no update, pieces of information were programmed to disappear from the board. Both flights still delayed, now both without a time of arrival. It was 11.30pm. Would the regulations allow planes to land after midnight?

Wasn't there always a curfew? Even the airport staff thought the remaining faithful were being optimistic.

Jeder cast over a glance at Hakan's assistant. He looked grumpy but thought that the overtime just about made it worthwhile. He was beginning to doubt that the project would be completed that night and was resigned to giving up most of his Saturday and Sunday as well. More time away from his son.

'Why were these bloody foreigners in the country anyway? Turkey can get on fine without them. It has always managed in the past. What on earth can this jumped-up Englishman teach us that we don't already know?   With his stupid English magazine bought for half my daily wages. He didn't even have the courtesy to offer me one of his cigarettes. Since what time have I been awake?'

Jeder was on the point of going to departures. He'd need to negotiate the border guard and hope that he wouldn't cross check Jeder's name and passport number to a hand-written list of grounded foreigners that was sellotaped onto the inside of his kiosk window. To his surprise, at the airport so far, there had been no restraint at all; he hadn't been pulled aside into a small office for an interview and his overnight bag had been given no more than a cursory glance.

An airport official approached him.

'Come with me please. *Buyrun'*. He was taken through the steel doors in arrivals. Straight through, that was good. Maybe Jeder was lucky with the timing, a change of shifts; maybe it was a bad Friday evening for the border patrol guards but a good one for Jeder.

Abruptly, Jeder was directed to take a sharp right turn and forced into one of the search rooms.

1 1

FEW OF THEM KNOW

Nurettin met Javier at the usual place in the Retiro, on the bench underneath the Mimosa tree by the crystal palace. Javier said he had a proposition for him and Nurettin didn't need a second invitation.

'You keep coming back then?'

'Are you surprised?', Nurettin joined Javier on the bench. The grey streaks around Javier's temples weren't evident; Nurettin wasn't sure whether this was due to the application of some ginger colouring or whether storm clouds above his head had been dispersed and somehow Javier was recapturing his youth.

'It's only been two weeks. I'm surprised you're still coming...I thought Turkey no longer wants to join the EU, now you're becoming so big and self-sufficient'.

'I think we still have interests in common, don't we? Agreements still in existence and promises to keep?'

'Don't you have responsibilities to be boss of your own region with your own view of the world?'

'The danger is you're becoming too fat and complacent. Not you personally of course'.

'*Dime algo bueno*'.

Nurettin tried to relax, despite the missing bench slat. The fact that it was 18 degrees, even on a November day, helped. The sky was totally blue. His curly black hair stayed in place, shining in the sun, 'Winter is never better than this'.

'Do you really think with all that money you're going to make you'll ever be able to buy back your soul?', Javier made shifting movements on the uncomfortable bench so as not to be too close to Nurettin.

'What do you mean?' A group of five *chicas* passed behind them. With their washer woman banter and their gin-soaked cigarette voices they could have been taken for women in their fifties or sixties. As they came into his ninety degree view, Nurettin was surprised to see they were in their early twenties, maybe some of them even in their late teens. He reflected that they had lost a generation somewhere but their camaraderie gave a warm feeling that they had secured their grip on gaiety from their youth.

'*El metodo Ponzi, una estafa de caracter piramidal que consiste en retribuir los benficios de unos inversores con el dinero de otros*'.

Nurettin stood up, as if the word 'Ponzi' had stuck a knife in his back, 'You know the court held in the cathedral in Valencia, where local farmers gather to talk about the water supply for the irrigation of their crops. They have been meeting there for over one hundred years. This is the only court whose decisions are recognised in Spain outside those made by state courts. This is the kind of meeting I imagine presiding over with an international scope…a court whose decisions in Turkey are recognised outside!'

'*¡Cien años antes del corralito global!*' Javier remained on the bench, a little more slumped than he'd been when Nurettin was sitting next to him.

'As supplies dry up, just think of the impact on agriculture and industry. About 70% of fresh water supplies are used in farming. Power generators, semiconductor manufacturers, the food and clothing industry, just think how dependent they all are on water supply. I can think of 22 countries that are reliant on other countries for their water'. Nurettin stood watching the *chicas* from behind as they disappeared into the distance, not before they mocked him, trying to persuade him they possessed plenty of frivolity after all.

'*¡Veintidos paises en el mundo!* Spread the impact across lots of countries. That way, nobody is hurt too much.' Javier began to think that he preferred to be on the beach at Cañabal in Valencia ; cleaning the fisherman's' creels made from reed, wicker or oleander. He imagined scraping out the seaweed and other muck from the semi-spherical creels and depositing the unwanted collections from the sea onto the sand at the water's edge. Then, returning to his boat and painstakingly fitting two newly cleaned creels together, joining them at their widest point to form a cage, closing one end, applying the bait inside the cage, fitting the funnel at the other end and then, once out at sea, lowering the cages to the bottom of the sea and waiting for the lobster and crab catch.

He looked casual but quietly competent in his straw hat and simple working clothes. He was seduced by the bright Valencian sky and the intense blue waters as the boat moved further and further away from the Cañabal shore. He was enchanted by this simple existence uncluttered by offers of money. Perhaps his past aberrations gave him the excuse to hide himself away in an idyllic fisherman's existence in Valencia.

'Your grandfather helped on the project to redirect the Turia', Nurettin swivelled round to assess the level at which he was being the butt of Javier's jokes, 'that was in 1957. Here we are, almost half a century later, with a lot more knowledge about climatic impacts on water supply and we know a little more about engineering'.

'*¡No me siento bien!*', Javier held one hand up from his crouched position.

'What's that?' Nurettin was now staring back into the space from where the *chicas* had disappeared,

'I am not my grandfather. Let me give you some perspective', Javier finally looked towards Nurettin. 'The project to divert water from the Ebro to supply the area around Valencia, Almeria and Murcia was conservatively budgeted at 4.2 billion Euros.'

'That's the size of the pot', Nurettin smiled. 'On my side I have developers and politicians with fingers in all sorts of pies. If you provide me with that amount of fund I can promise a 200% return in five years; and, as you mentioned Ponzi earlier, no end of people do not realise they have a bad deal until a few years later. There are no international laws defining or regulating the use of shared water resources'.

'*No me atrae mucho lo del viaje a Turquia*', Javier muttered to himself.

'What's that?' Nurettin asked, taking a little delay before he managed to work out what Javier might have been saying, 'Don't worry, you won't have to spend much time in Istanbul, I know you don't like it'.

'You're wrong, I find Istanbul fascinating, what I find abhorrent is the whole concept of what we are about to do, your morals and what drives you.'

'Well, not everyone is perfect, no?'

'I made a few mistakes, I won't dwell on them, but I don't want to re-create the same thought processes that led me there in the first place. You haven't made any earth-shattering mistakes yet, but don't you realise you are just about to?'

'Well there are many details we still have to discuss, there are things I can change if you find it difficult to stay faithful to the plan, as it is at the moment'.

Javier arched his back like a tomcat trying to scare off a persistently barking small terrier '¿Y la posolagía? ¿Cuántos comprimídos per día?'

'What are you saying?'

'Recently, I am more involved in ethical projects. A friend of mine who I have known since student days has a water consultancy company...'.

Nurettin's ears pricked.

'...but you won't be able to corrupt him', Javier intervened before Nurettin could say anything.

'He advises big companies...', Javier tried to continue.

'He knows big companies ? He could replace Jeder'.

'Oh, Jeder. Whatever happened to his big rice project? Where was it? Oh yes, Trabzon, el ciudad portuaria del mar Negro.' Javier hoped Nurettin's face might show some signs of remorse but it remained expressionless. 'But let me finish, the person I know

214

advises big companies how to save water. Just look at the impact that the biofuel industry is having on water consumption. It takes 2,500 litres of water to make 1 litre of biofuel'.

'But that is not his business, right?'

'No, it's more straightforward than that. The volumes these companies use are big. So it's about re-using waste water for dirty jobs that need heavy amounts of water but the water quality for that use doesn't need to be so good. Simple things like dust suppression. It's also about using closed-loop water systems for industrial cooling. And, at a more basic level, it's about reducing the frequency of water-cleaning industrial equipment, changing cleaning patterns.'

'And plugging leaks..?'

'Yeah, plugging leaks.'

"And this interests you?"

'We know how expensive water is going to be, he is able to charge his clients for his services, not based on today's cost of water, but on water saved, calculated by using a forecasted rate for the cost of water in 2 years time. This is where you come in!'

'What about the competition? He can't be the only one in this business. Where's my commission? By next year he will be able to charge at the prospective cost of water in 4 year's time! Jeder never told me about this kind of charging model!' Nurettin looked like he'd been short-changed.

'Jeder's pricing structures never allowed for the kind of cross subsidy mechanism that allows the poor people to access water at an appropriate quality and at an affordable price. As these people move from the arid lowlands to the moister uplands and hills trying to find water to support agriculture for subsistence, there is growing pressure on the upland environment. This puts at risk the quality, quantity and regularity of the current and potential river-based supplies and, in turn, adds to the cost of water treatment. Anyway, if you're interested I can introduce you to Manu next time?'

'Yes, I would certainly like to meet him'.

'I know you always like to meet some place where we can't be overheard but maybe I can arrange a quiet corner of a restaurant? Rather than freezing our nuts out here in January.'

'I'll think about it. I have to go now; it's an early flight back to Istanbul. I'll be in touch'.

Javier waved Nurettin off in the direction of the Hotel Wellington.

It was still only mid-morning and, as Nurettin had a few minutes to kill before his airport taxi, he switched on the television in his hotel room. He scrolled through endless Spanish-speaking channels before eventually arriving at the TRT International news channel. On cue, the top-of- the-hour news bulletin flashed up a headline 'TURKEY ACCUSED OF BLEEDING SYRIA DRY'. Footage of vast areas of cracked mud was interspersed with hollowed-eyed villagers proffering empty palms. The caption at the foot of the screen read 'WATER SHORTAGES THREATEN THE LIVELIHOOD OF MILLIONS OF PEOPLE'.

The news item didn't linger for too long on these images before showing a short interview with an outraged government spokesman in Damascus, confronted by microphones and flashlights. After a couple of brief exchanges, the Syrian diplomat was quickly gesticulating, shouting and pointing at the TRT reporter; she only lightly recoiled, pushing her microphone back towards the politician, only for him to turn and walk away. The coverage then switched to a man from Ankara giving a calm and considered response to a similar opening question, indicating that the situation would be reviewed.

The bedside phone ringing diverted Nurettin's attention.

'Do you know what just happened?' Arzu's was the only voice that immediately made Nurettin feel good. 'Someone called me out of the blue saying I shouldn't leave the apartment for the whole of tomorrow. Of course, he wouldn't say who he was. But when I asked him what would happen if I *did* go out, he said *you* would be killed. Do you think it's a hoax?' Arzu was unusually animated.

'Call the police'.

'It's about *you*, not me', and then Arzu raised her voice, incredulous that Nurettin was taking this intrusion so casually, still deploying his default trait of being in control, 'what do you think happens the day after?'

'You're the one who is being threatened'.

'It's all over the news here, have you seen it?'

'Yes, I'm watching it now. They're trying to interview people. There, look!' Nurettin gestured to the screen, assuming Arzu was looking at the same scene. 'Nobody in Ankara is saying anything to the reporters. So, it could be passed over as western hysteria.'

'You hope'.

'It's a long time since western governments have been concerned about Syria'.

'What about the aid agencies, they have people in situ, it's their reports that are being seized on'.

'The Turkish government will not accept responsibility for this. What was his accent?'

'He was Turkish'.

'He's just trying it on'.

'Yes, but I am here, you're in Spain. I'm going to call Mehmet. If I'm still alive on Thursday I think I'll go and stay with my sister'.

'Have you checked he hasn't already called her?', there was still no hint of urgency or alarm in Nurettin's voice.

'You're the first person I rang, he only called me ten minutes ago, I'm lucky to find you in the hotel'.

'My flight is at 1.30'.

'You're not racing back then?'

'This is the next available flight, if I leave right now'.

1 2

NORMAL PRACTICE

Nurettin swung his car into the underground car park along the street from the block of flats where he lived. After returning from Madrid in the early evening, he had dinner with Ilker in a Bebek café. His Spanish restaurant rule on not discussing plans still did not apply in Istanbul.

'Have you *not* seen the news yet?', Ilker assumed this must have reached Madrid.

'This will pass over', Nurettin responded dryly.

'How?'

'Megaphone diplomacy will prevail'.

'Gunboat..?'

Ilker was where Nurettin wanted to be; he was ahead of him and Nurettin wanted to analyse why and how this had happened every time he caught sight of his *Istanbullu* friend. Ilker had an engine inside that drove him in a mechanical and unemotional way.

Ilker was the same age as Nurettin but it hadn't been his childhood in Izmir that had held Nurettin back. Istanbul families across three generations had been taught to kick away faith, but without it they faced basic questions of their own existence. Secular children had been produced; these were polished and aspiring Western European sons and daughters, but spiritually they were struggling. Nurettin saw this as weakness in some of his Istanbullu friends but as an outsider he felt unaffected by it and stronger for it.

'So, how was your trip?' Nurettin wanted to quickly deflect the topic of conversation away from his difficulties.

Ilker had just returned from Africa and began with his trademark rallying cry, 'Ethiopia is the water tower of Africa, Getachew says so!'

Nurettin was outwardly congratulatory and encouraging, but inwardly depressed when he heard about Ilker's latest venture in Ethiopia. Ilker had been buying up tracts of land, where there was access to water, and contracting cheap labour to work it; he said he was not taking land that already belonged to Ethiopian farmers, although it could take years to sort out whether the same piece of land had been sold two or three times already.

'What's changed?'

'Nothing,' Ilker quoted the same statistics that Nurettin had seen issued by the Ethiopian government. 'Still about 15% of the country's fertile land is already used by subsistence farmers and only a further 5% has been sold to foreign investors; not just to Turkish investors like me but also to the Chinese and the Saudis'.

'And the other 80?'

'Well the 20% sum, and the 5% within that, is still probably the ceiling because there is livestock to graze and the rest lies fallow for a reason; already the international agencies are involved with the state government to try to prevent nutrient depletion and erosion. The 80% is known about, it isn't empty'.

Ilker had previously tried and failed to interest Nurettin, who was so flush with cash since the Tulon co-operation. At least, that's what Ilker believed. A more remote source for Ilker was Nurettin's friend, Cengiz, who was supposedly seeking a home for his development bank funds on precisely this kind of project.

In the two countries he had visited in sub-Saharan Africa, Nurettin only saw some of the world's poorest communities vulnerable to the effects of falling water tables, drought and flooding. Rainwater was needed to be collected and then to be used for drinking, for planting trees and for easing the work of digging trenches and pits. Although 85% of the Nile originated in Ethiopia, the country was using so little of it; an almost inverse situation to Turkey's control of the Euphrates and Tigris. In Ethiopia time had stood still, in Turkey certainly not.

'As I told you before, Cengiz has always said that loans could be set up for the right projects but right now those projects had to be based in Turkey, not abroad'. Nurettin continued, 'I told you about my conversations with Yıldırım at Tulon, have you still not investigated the hydroelectric power projects?' Nurettin was hoping Ilker would meet with delegates from the Italian firm that was involved in the reservoir construction, but it seems that Ilker had veered off into another direction.

'The food my farms will produce can be exported to Turkey, that way Turkey can reduce its own agricultural output and conserve its own water. But I'll still need financing. You know, it's very topical right now; the EU is worried about how subsidy reforms could make them more vulnerable to foreign imports. Well, they should spare a thought for the sugar workers in Ethiopia and how the subsidy in EU and world sugar has been killing off the Ethiopian farms. I'm going to help reverse that trend in Ethiopia'.

'How much exactly are you going to be charged for your water, on the farms you'll have in Ethiopia?', Nurettin suspected that these rates would be very high, representing a tax for land grabbing. He had always accused Ilker of taking on more than he could cope with.

'We use very little water; we have a specialist Dutch company that has mastered techniques to minimise the use of water for irrigation in Africa. Just think about the increase in crop yields we can generate in just a few years'.

'What about subventions from the local state government?' Nurettin had almost finished his dish of *levrek* whilst Ilker was only about half way through his *palamut*.

'Not easy and certainly not quick to procure. At times there are conflicting priorities. For instance, sometimes state governments will offer incentives to potential investors in biofuels which use a water intensive crop such as sugar cane on a vast scale'.

'You are up against de-forestation and torrential rainfalls when it does come. Whole communities and farms can be devastated at a stroke. All your work can be buried overnight in that region. Year-on-year annual yields will plummet. Where is your insurance?'

'You believe the four inches rise in sea levels by the end of this new century? Our partners have funding from Denmark's international development agency and are hopeful that UK's DFID will also contribute; our proposals need to be nimble and prolific to ensure we are at the front of the queue with attractive propositions'. Ilker was becoming a little more distant and wondered how much he should tell Nurettin about what he was doing.

For his part, Nurettin didn't know him that well; it had been an easy but never a deep friendship.

'Finish up, and then let's go'. Nurettin went over to the back of the café to settle his bill.

Ilker rose to leave and put on his raincoat. Nurettin followed him to the door of the cafe as if he was the owner. Ilker grabbed Nurettin's arm above the elbow and asked him with mock concern 'What about your friend?'

Nurettin jostled Ilker outside while still holding the door ajar, 'Oh, he's being held.....as an example of Western corruption'.

Ilker's hair and face were soon soaked under the cold sleeting rain and he looked down to the floor with a wry smile, not knowing whether to be sympathetic or to laugh out loud.

Nurettin loitered alone at the Bebek cafe, a long time after Ilker had left, trying to work out why his own scheme was never going to work.

The Euphrates had already dried up in Iraq. Skiffs lay dry and splintering on its banks. Iraq's agricultural lands could no longer support wheat, barley and rice growing, but Nurettin had convinced himself that this was not of his doing. The Iraqi government had ordered its farmers in Nasiriyah to stop growing rice. The marshland residents had started to move on into the towns.

Parts of the Euphrates and Tigris were cracked mud. International newspaper headlines and television news bulletins reported with equal outrage that supplies from the Tigris had been cut off to Iraq and, supplies from the Euphrates had been cut off to Syria and therefore Iraq, 'through necessity' according to Turkish governmental sources.

Nurettin slumped in his car with his head on the steering wheel. He turned off the wipers, the lights and then the ignition. Insulated from the sleet outside.

He remained in the dark in his car in the underground car park with only the cracking sound of his car's hot engine cooling and the surge and trickle of water waste pipes disgorging from the apartments above to puncture the total silence. At least he didn't have to smell anymore those rat and cat odours and the stale water stench from that basement corridor when he went to visit Jeder.

He was no longer a god masquerading as a man. He kept seeing sandstorms. He cursed Javier for his procrastination, he cursed Jeder for his intransigence. He cursed his wife. How in just five years they went from people who believed they were perfectly matched kindred spirits, to trying to deliberately avoid each other, to finally reaching the point of dreading seeing each other. They continued this charade only because neither of them knew how to finish it.

'How was your day?' was Nurettin's ironic opening gambit as soon as he was inside the hallway of his apartment, already opening his mail. There was no immediate reply from Arzu. Nurettin opened up his bank statement expecting to see the latest payment from Tulon but there was nothing. When he came into the bedroom Arzu was there, lying in bed.

'How was yours?' She had been smouldering since her call with Nurettin finished, but she was not surprised that it had taken him so long to return from Madrid.

'Ilker is still being stubborn', Nurettin sat down in his bedroom armchair, relaxed in his home environment, 'he needs more funds for his Ethiopian project'.

'Did that ever start?'

'Sort of....but the evening didn't work out, as I couldn't persuade him to join the meeting with SCRITALO and I really need him. How was your day?' Arzu didn't answer. It was almost as if Nurettin had been programmed to forget all about their earlier call. He stood up and left to go to the bathroom.

Since the call, Arzu had started to re-examine the rest of her life and was not overly delighted with the prospects. Unhappiness, that had hitherto appeared superficial, all of a sudden felt very deep. She wanted to be positive when Nurettin returned to the room.

She pulled back the bedclothes, went over to open the curtains and looked through the rain-specked window to the street below. There was no traffic, nor was there any audible street chatter. All sounds were muffled and snowflakes began to fall. The call to prayer was over an hour ago. She couldn't identify that she was in Istanbul but she was in a room, stuck at the end of a tunnel. She knew no one like her. Where she had been and what she had done had always been a positive choice by her. Up until now.

She felt she was being viewed with deep suspicion by men around her, although her female colleagues were sympathetic; but a lot of her friends she was no longer close to, as all they seemed to talk about was their children or being a mother. She knew what she wanted to say to Nurettin once he had returned to the room, 'When you don't have a happy ending you need to know someone is there with you, sharing the pain'.

Nurettin didn't come back to the room and left the flat shortly before midnight. As he came out of the front door of the apartment block, fresh snow was falling and he looked up into the white sky illuminating the tops of the buildings around. He stumbled on a large heavy solid object on the door step and fell head-first out onto the street, his coat sleeves and hands all covered in sludge. As he sprawled over the object, he knew it was another body. When you're that intimate with a body, you're able to have a good guess at its weight; somewhere between 70 and 80 kilos.

Once he stood up and turned around, he could see the obstruction in the half light. It was a male body, just. It could have been a Chechnya guerrilla leader's mutilated corpse; flipped up blood spattered clothes covered the top half of the body and obscured the head and shoulders. Contrasting with the settling new snow in the wider area, a halo of fresh deep red blood on the tarmac formed where the top of his head should have been. The fact that his trousers had been pulled down his thighs was presumably intended by his killers to make a point. Nurettin flinched and turned away, but even if he had looked at that body for a nanosecond the detailed image was always going to stay with him. When he turned back again, he could only look as far as the blood puddle steadily increasing its coverage and shattering his fantasy that he was standing in a cave in the mountains south of Grozny.

He crossed to the other side of the road. A fizzing sound and a rush of wind through his hair coincided with a crack noise on the side of a building up the street and a group of grazing pigeons under cover from the snow scattered into the grey sky.

He crouched down. He couldn't tell from which direction the bullet had come. He wasn't going to try to go back into his apartment. He started to run along the middle of the road, slipped on the slush and crashed down; the impact ripped one trouser leg, grazed his knee and left his entire right side totally sodden.

He stood up again, this time gingerly and started walking slowly. If they wanted to shoot him now, he would be an even easier target. A busier street came into view, and he saw plenty of cars and a taxi pass. He started running again, whilst trying to look back, and attempting to stay balanced in the slush; he couldn't see anybody behind, but did not have anything like 180 degree vision. He reached the adjacent road and walked down the pavement to find an empty bus shelter; no night buses would stop at this one. No taxi came for a few minutes. His right leg was beginning to seize up in a combination of clotted blood and the cold. Then an empty taxi came into view. He ran out into the road and waved it down, shouted through the open side window. 'Çamlıca'. The driver nodded but, as Nurettin closed the taxi door, one side of the glass on the bus shelter was shattered. Nurettin had one final look around through the iced-up window as best he could but couldn't see anybody. The driver didn't hear the bang nor notice the glass splinters all over the pavement and, once Nurettin was inside, he drove off.

Hakan was still up and opened the front door of his ground floor apartment in Çamlıca, astonished to be greeting anyone at this time of night. The palm of Nurettin's right hand was also cut so he kept it in his coat pocket. He tried to look as cold and bedraggled as he could with his left coat sleeve ripped and that arm, exposed from his elbow downwards, turning blue.

'You can't come in'. Hakan looked at the dishevelled state of Nurettin, whose optimistic face did not elicit any sympathy.

'You need to help me for a few hours. I can't go home'.

'Come round to the back'.

Hakan led Nurettin round to the back of his apartment block, then down a narrow staircase with uneven steps to a below-ground entrance in the back street. Before he pushed open the door, Hakan turned to Nurettin, 'what is it you want?'

'I need a ticket on the first flight out to Damascus. You need to arrange me a taxi and find me some lira and dollars. A lot.'

13

OVERSTAYED

There was no early morning plane to Damascus so Hakan had arranged an internal flight to Gaziantep. It was late that evening by the time Nurettin reached an isolated village two hours drive from Ar Raqqah; he'd had to transfer from Gaziantep via Birecik by road and then across the border. Around Ar Raqqah, his driver had said that the intention was for low-cost housing to sprout up over the previous twenty years or so. Nurettin just saw many incomplete housing blocks with started, but unfinished, service roads like failed arteries, and untidy random circular gaps in the ground like bomb holes. He couldn't help feel apprehensive about venturing through Kurdish areas, something he would never do in Turkey itself. This was the place that Ilker had recommended he go see a real Syrian village, with no concrete in sight.

He was to be put up by an uncle of Ilker, who lived with his wife and sister. When he eventually reached the village, it seemed from the pick-up's headlights that there were some reinforced concrete and cement block houses, most of them single-storey. Ilker's uncle house, however, was a rammed earth building. Speaking good Turkish, he greeted Nurettin and showed him inside the building, singling out the wood ceiling beams as a feature whilst he leant against one of two large wooden vertical floor posts that looked as though they might support a second-storey construction.

This prompted Nurettin to try to break the ice with 'Nobody pays too much attention to the roof unless it leaks'. Ilker's uncle didn't understand him but was convinced any joke was at his expense, probably on account of his nephew once describing him as miserly.

There were two big rooms, one family room with a wood-burning stove and the other a guest room, which was cold and felt a little unloved and unused. There was no glazing in any of the windows in the house, but in the guest room there were rugs shoved against the window openings to shield the inhabitants from the cold nights.

Ilker's uncle led Nurettin back outside. He couldn't have been much over fifty-five, but looked about seventy with his lined face, grey hair and moustache and stooped posture. Nurettin struggled to find any resemblance in him to Ilker, neither in looks nor character. He couldn't recall whether Ilker had said he was a teacher or a farmer. He didn't wear a keffiyeh nor any other headwear.

'We used to have about 300 acres of wheat grown in this area, now it's less than half that', Ilker's uncle was immediately hostile towards Nurettin, 'it used to be cultivated farmland all around here. Now a lot of that land is desert. Flour is scarce. We used to export wheat but now we're importers'.

'What happened?'

'They say that water in Syria has dried up through waste and overuse but we know better', Ilker's uncle stooped a little lower and Nurettin wondered how long it had been since he was actively involved in farming. Nurettin wasn't about to fill in the blanks about the reasons for the drought.

'It hasn't always been like this', Ilker's uncle tried to straighten his back but winced as he did so. 'The farming communities are breaking up. Lots of farmers have left the country. The government is totally unprepared for the impact of this'.

'Lack of food or skilled people leaving?'

'There's that. I'm more worried about the irreparable damage. A lot of the ancient irrigation systems have collapsed and underground water sources dried up. Of course, the worst hit areas are where the Kurdish communities are. Look what's happened there. This is not a normal drought, this is permanent.' Ilker's uncle, seeing there was not going to be any admission of guilt, went back inside leaving Nurettin to stare into the dark.

Ilker's uncle, his wife, his sister and three children must have been all together in one room while Nurettin slept in the other room. He didn't really sleep at all. He wasn't used to sleeping on the ground although the floor looked well-made from a combination of compacted soil, gravel and straw. It was very hard with no covering, so Nurettin took down the rug from the window and lay on that although he felt both hip bones and his knee wound, whichever side he chose. What continually kept waking him up were dogs barking nervously throughout the night. Once one started, others would follow. Smaller dogs, then bigger dogs, high-pitched and then deeper barks and sustained howls, until there was quite a cacophony. The momentum was only stalled when an irate owner shouted down or slapped a dog, and then other owners repeated the two-pronged approach with the latter action being more effective in choking off the clamour. It would be light about 6.30.

Even at 7.00 Nurettin was shocked by the stifling heat, surprising for the time of year; it should have been about 15 degrees centigrade. Hakan's wool trousers just about fitted him but probably wouldn't survive the trip. He'd brought with him bottled water and was embarrassed that his hosts would not partake of it. Even though he thought he had ample supplies he was glad that he intended to leave the village later that morning for the arduous return trip. He did not join in any prayers, but did not feel he needed to excuse himself for his perfidy. There was no school that day for the children; the family could only afford to send the eldest child, who was ten, to school one day a week. Ilker's aunt added that she could not provide the children with two meals a day and could only keep them in one set of clothes, medicine was unaffordable.

In the morning, Ilker's uncle had disappeared and it was his wife who showed Nurettin the complex of the deep wells that tapped into the underground water table. She was much younger than her husband, probably not yet in her thirties. She was bright and outgoing and Nurettin felt comfortable for the first time in Syria. She spoke in Kurmanji, and with some Turkish interspersed, Nurettin was able to follow what she was saying. The surrounding communities were meant to be sustained by the series of wells and shafts that only gave out excess water without disrupting the ground water level. These water sources held together the diverse ethnic communities, thousands of people who had migrated there over the years after their own sources of water dried up. Except now these sources were drying up, despite the best efforts of a water engineer who had visited them from Pakistan. Ilker's aunt said that the Pakistan engineer left them with the remark that 'they can keep digging more and more holes, deeper and deeper, but eventually all these water sources will just dry up, there is no more water'. She then said that 'our struggle to obtain any water is just another price of poverty.' It was not as if any of the adjoining villages had any better access to water. The engineer had also told them that, as the levels fell, the nitrates became more concentrated and the water would eventually become too dangerous to drink. He felt his remarks had been wasted, as these villagers were not going to move, unless a natural disaster made them.

About 10am there was a fracas outside one of the huts; one of the village elders was shouting at others and pointing into the distance, from where one of the villagers had just arrived. There was what looked like a dust storm in the distance. Nurettin assumed this was the time to go inside and batten down the hatches. Instead the panting, out- of- breath, young man gestured to the matriarch of a household that she should collect her belongings and kids and flee. She started to argue with him, hands on hips. He was affronted by her challenge and the village elder needed to intervene to reinforce the young man's instruction. At least this is what Nurettin believed was the gist of the altercation, because he did not understand all the words of this dialect.

Nurettin fixed his gaze on the dust clouds about a couple of kilometres away, to try to fathom whether they were moving closer. He thought he heard primeval earth shifting sounds which reminded him of the Istanbul earthquake from 1999, but could not recall this particular part of Syria being on a fault line. He looked for heavy machinery, although realised he was very unlikely to see large earth moving diggers or heavy plant in this part of the country. Meanwhile there was another disturbance behind him in the house. The children were resisting the orders to leave and the young man had run inside the house to snatch the eldest boy by his right shoulder and arm and pulled him out into the open, with such force that Nurettin feared the poor boy's shoulder would be dislocated, as his mother shouted at the other two kids. Once the young man relented, the eldest kid protested he knew best. He shouted boldly that there had been sand storms before, this was no different, he was not frightened.

The young man tugged violently again at the kid's arm, then started shaking it, saying 'Don't be stupid. We've seen whole villages buried in sand'.

Their attention was diverted as dogs scattered in different directions away from the village. At the same time, groups of people were running and stumbling towards the village from the direction of the dust cloud, as if they were

239

desperately trying to keep ahead of a noxious gas. Some were bloodied with their clothes ripped, some were badly incapacitated and shuffled or limped. The cloud accelerated and consumed them, several disappeared from view and one or two at the front stumbled and fell flat on their faces.

Then there was a prehistoric moan from the ground behind the series of concrete buildings, lean-tos and huts that comprised the main part of the village. From deep below it sounded as if parts of the earth were grinding against each other. A significant amount of displacement of soil and sand seeped down into large gaps that appeared now only about 50 metres away. Nurettin realised he had no power to resist what was about to happen. The bold boy, free from the young man's grip, screamed with anticipation, as if he was going to charge into the waves of the sea. Instead, he and his siblings started to run off towards the approaching dust cloud. Soon Nurettin was enveloped by the mist formed by the sand, he lost his footing, steadied himself for a moment and was then completely spun off his feet, entered into a trance in which he felt he was in an apogaeic fall. Momentarily he regained consciousness and realised he was now falling with gravity into a yawning gap in the earth.

His instinct was to protect his head at the risk of limbs being broken. He fell but fortunately not as far or as deeply as he had first feared; nothing felt broken but he was wedged. The sound and vibrations had lasted less than a minute and there was a pause. Less than ten seconds later there was a further scream from the earth's core and movement and he fell again, this time feet first, what felt like at least five metres, certainly far enough to break his legs or worse, so he thought. Then he lost consciousness.

When an 80kg boulder falls on your face there is no reason to think you can survive. There wasn't time to think about the world he had left behind; what he could have done differently or better; no time to create an image of his father; dismay that he'd never proved himself to his father; that his father died believing him to be worthless; no time to explain to people what he had done or why he had done it; that he couldn't right the things he had done wrong, so that people would think better of him. There was insufficient time to consider that his body was so mutilated that no one would know or care who he was. No time to taste or spit out crushed teeth, meshed with blood, flesh, stones, grit and dirt.

When he imagined he came to, he couldn't move or speak but thought he could see. Attempted instructions from his brain to the rest of his body moved nothing. Somehow from an angle through a shaft of light he saw the surface above. The village resembled a wasteland. Buildings, even the rammed earth home, had collapsed or disappeared altogether. Beams protruded out of the earth and rubble at strange angles like broken legs. Anybody still alive must have been stuck in cellars which hadn't been filled in by the earth. He thought he made out someone shouting from the surface down to those below and trying to move mounds of rubble, stone by stone. The shouts were becoming muffled and distant as if blood was filling his only remaining functioning eardrum. Someone was trying to reach what was left of a well. Water was needed, potable water; no kind of receptacle could be found. Those trapped underneath the debris would need water, above all, until they could be freed. Any other survivors must have feared a tertiary collapse; no one would want to stand next to any remaining structure that hadn't been flattened.

Any tracks or roads that had existed to join communities together would now be untraceable, as if they had been clinically target bombed. What means of transport and livestock, including the donkeys that carried people and goods up and down the unmade tracks, that had once existed to help livelihoods, had now vanished in a return of development and civilisation to pre-history.

Glossary

Bey — A formal term of respect used for an older man or a man in a position of high authority.

Cılbır — Poached eggs coated in garlic-flavoured yogurt, butter and sage.

Dolmuş — A shared minibus taxi.

Gecekondular — Cheap, illegal dwellings constructed very quickly (literally overnight) by people migrating from rural areas into the big cities.

Hamsi sarması — Anchovies wrapped in vine leaves.

Hanım — A formal term of respect used for an older woman or a woman in a position of high authority.

Iskele — A landing place for small boats for passengers to embark and disembark along the shore line.

Kuru incir receli — Dried fig jam popular in Western Anatolia.

Kuzu ve anya yahnisi — Lamb and quince stew.

Lahmacun — Anatolian street food consisting of a thin dough base coated with minced lamb, tomatoes, onions, chillies and garlic.

Levrek — Sea bass.

Palamut — Bonito.

15123243R00148

Printed in Great Britain
by Amazon